A
PUBLIC
SPACE
No. 31

T013140?

This is an issue of weather and misinterpretation, and the unexpected patterns created by these natural forces.
—Brigid Hughes

WEBED LEATHER

FOR EAGLE OTTAWA — c.1958

Dorothy Liebes, sample card for Eagle
Ottawa Leather Corp. 1958.

TABLE OF CONTENTS

A PUBLIC SPACE
(ISSN 1558-965X;
ISBN 9798985976953)
IS PUBLISHED BY
A PUBLIC SPACE
LITERARY PROJECTS, INC.
PO BOX B
NEW YORK, NY 10159.
PRINTED IN TK.
ISSUE 31, ©2023
A PUBLIC SPACE
LITERARY PROJECTS, INC.
POSTMASTER PLEASE
SEND CHANGES OF
ADDRESS TO A PUBLIC
SPACE, PO BOX B, NEW
YORK, NY 10159.

**A PUBLIC SPACE
IS SUPPORTED
IN PART BY**

**A PUBLIC SPACE IS A
PROUD MEMBER OF**
The Community of
Literary Magazines and
Presses

[clmp]

No. 31　　A PUBLIC SPACE

EDITOR
Brigid Hughes

POETRY EDITOR
Brett Fletcher Lauer

COVER DESIGN
Janet Hansen

EDITORIAL FELLOW
Ruby Wang

ASSOCIATE EDITORS
Sarah Blakley-
Cartwright
Sidik Fofana
Taylor Michael
Laura Preston

COPY EDITOR
Anne McPeak

READERS
Joshua Craig, Zoe
Davis, Julia Ring,
Klein Voorhees, Alex
Yeranossian

INTERNS
Theia Chatelle, Lara
Treisman

**CONTRIBUTING
EDITORS**
Annie Coggan
Martha Cooley
Edwin Frank
Mark Hage
John Haskell
Yiyun Li
Fiona Maazel
Ayana Mathis
Robert Sullivan
Antoine Wilson

**INTERNATIONAL
CONTRIBUTING
EDITORS**
Dorthe Nors
(Denmark)
Natasha Randall
(England)
Motoyuki Shibata
(Japan)

EDITOR AT LARGE
Elizabeth Gaffney

BOARD OF DIRECTORS
Katherine Bell
Charles Buice
Rimjhim Dey
Elizabeth Gaffney
Brigid Hughes
Yiyun Li
Robert Sullivan

ADVISORY BOARD
Robert Casper
Fiona McCrae
James Meader

**FOUNDING
BENEFACTOR**
Deborah Pease
(1943-2014)

SUBSCRIPTIONS
Postpaid subscription
for 3 issues: $36 in
the United States;
$54 in Canada;
$66 internationally.
Subscribe at
www.apublicspace.org
or send a check to the
address below.

CONTACT
For general queries,
please email
general@apublicspace.org
or call (718) 858-8067.
A Public Space
is located at
PO Box B
New York, NY 10159.

Maiko Takeda, Atmospheric Reentry

CORINNA VALLIANATOS
A LOT OF GOOD IT DOES BEING IN THE UNDERWORLD

———

Says an unsavory character in *The Stranger,* which I'm rereading to see how it strikes me now. By underworld, he means a group of petty criminals, but I think the sentiment applies to the place, too. It's not damnation that sends you there. It's the instinct for return.

When I heard that my friend was dead, I thought back to our exchange of texts the week before. We had planned to meet at a fish restaurant for lunch and her death seemed impossible with this plan unrealized. I believed in plans, in the adhesive property of the calendar, and while I could fathom a last-minute rescheduling—I deferred many social engagements—I could not fathom utter obviation, a voiding of the future as if it were a thing that could simply be stamped out. My friend lived on a mountain, and I lived in a valley. The restaurant was located roughly halfway between our houses. We had met there before. It had a scuffed black-and-white tile floor and milk-glass ceiling lamps, and the waiters wore broadcloth shirts and long black aprons. Despite its gesturing toward authenticity it could not shake its mantle of corporate arrangement, and we took solace in its anonymity. There, my friend ordered iced tea and broiled grouper while I ordered a dripping Kaiser roll sandwich. Lemon seeds in little puddles of water at the bases of our glasses.

That was five years ago at least. I'd told myself I'd contact her again when I had news to announce, an awful way of thinking about friendship, as if it existed only out in the open rather than in the underground life of shared sympathies. Eventually I did have some modest news, and I sent out a group email and she replied and that's how we fell back in touch.

After we arranged our lunch date we kept texting. We had both read Louise Glück's new collection of poems, her twelfth or thirteenth, and we discussed a particular poem, a particular line of that poem, You must ask yourself if you deceive yourself, which I'd read as You must ask yourself if you deserve yourself, and my friend had read as You must ask yourself if you desert yourself. How funny, how strange! we agreed, and then I said I thought my misreading got to the nature of womanhood itself, and my friend said her misreading was about the human desire for oblivion. To be a woman is more specific than to be a human, I responded. My friend did not reply, and that was the last I heard from her.

She was magnetic in the way of a being whose balance on earth is unsteady but the way she flaps across the axis, her arms out at her sides and bracelets rattling, utterly transfixing.

What feeling would you least want to elicit in others? I once asked her. Pity, my friend replied.

She never did. Admiration, concern, puzzlement, gratitude. Her students loved her very much.

We taught at the same university and then we didn't any longer—that's the simplest explanation for why we stopped seeing each other—but I admit it had become confusing to be with her, I sensed her hold on reality was slipping. She was always complimenting me, flattering me, making too much of small things. It was embarrassing and had, in fact, the opposite effect of what she intended, for I began to suspect myself of such demonstrable fragility that she thought I needed shoring up. I wonder now if she wasn't simply trying to deflect attention from herself, from the substance of her days. Eventually she would relay some event or drama, but the hyperbole continued, warping the proportions of what she said, pulling like an undertow against the stability of her story, a discernible chronology, a series of recognizable acts. I knew my friend thought what she was saying was true, and knew too that in some crucial way it was not. So when she told me about the time she abandoned her car at the side of a mountain road, and no one knew where she was, and the pills she had in her possession, I did not seize upon it. Instead, I exclaimed almost in awe at her confession, as if a monstrous feathered thing had brushed past me. That is to say, I understood her confession, but I pushed that understanding deep inside of me, just as I buried so many other unpleasant revelations.

Now, a month after her death, I stand in front of the building where my office is, among the careful, colorful shrubbery. Two young women walk past me wearing high-waisted jeans and indomitable expressions, a kick-assery somewhat undercut by their ardent clutching of their phones, and I think of my friend and how much pain we had ahead of us at that age, and how we didn't know it, and wonder what we'd have done differently had we known. Every young woman is captive to a painful future that she must not, cannot, see clearly, for if she did she would only try futilely to avoid it. It is futile even if her future is also filled with joy, as ours were. For the future doesn't end with joy—there is always a moment after, even if the joy is stronger than what comes next.

I stop reading for the classes I'm teaching and read poetry instead. Novels seem bloated and unnecessary, their tissue and ligaments, characters saying things. Whereas a poem is the declaration itself.

It's simple. It speaks. There is no need for continuity.

My friend slips from my mind for a day or two at a time and then returns from another angle, and I see her standing next to the elevator in the building where we taught, a different building on a different, duller campus, smiling, blinking behind her glasses, all blurry blue eyeliner and tall leather boots. The boots were catastrophically expensive, my friend told me. She stashed a flask in one of them. This was discovered later.

During this time, my friend emailed a manuscript to me, a memoir she'd written about the year she spent in Nova Scotia when she was twenty-two. I had difficulty understanding her poetry, which was highly referential and elaborate, each line so baroque something essential was obscured. Her memoir, however, was different. It was lucid, revelatory, filled with longing like a stream, a living, running thing. I encouraged her to publish it, but she never did. I suspect she was protecting her husband, for men are sensitive about old loves, or maybe she had other reasons, or maybe she did try to publish it and wasn't able to, but I don't think so.

Some words carry so much awareness inside them I can't read them at night, I can only read them during the day. For their awareness makes me aware. That's how I felt reading my friend's manuscript. That she was finally telling the truth, and the truth requires a response.

I decide to try to get the manuscript published posthumously. I look for it but I can't find it, and I realize it may be on an old laptop, a laptop that won't turn on but that I haven't recycled because of my fear it may still hold something important, an importance all the more significant because I can't get to the important thing, so I email her friend in another state to ask if she has a copy of it. My friend's friend takes a long time to reply, and when she does she says she doesn't have a copy of it, and that our friend never showed it to her or even mentioned it. It's as if she thinks I'm inventing the manuscript's existence, and I wonder if she's aggrieved that our friend shared something with me that she did not with her. That might've contributed to the slowness of her response, though she would if asked say that she was grieving, overwhelmed, overworked.

I email the editor of the press that published my friend's first book to see if she might have the manuscript. She does not. She says I should absolutely submit it if I find it, they open for submissions for three-and-a-half hours on January 4.

I don't know what people do all day long. This is the well of mystery I draw from.

I think about it a lot. The rhythms, rationales, ways of being of other people. My husband tells me not to try to understand, but I do. I can't help myself. The incredible mystery and loneliness of being someone else.

I wish I could've seen my friend age. Seen her as an old lady.

When I heard about her death I also heard that she was not married anymore.

Years ago, we got very drunk with our husbands and another couple. My husband and I had arranged for our son to stay with my parents for the night, and my friend's sons were staying with her parents, and the other couple did not yet have children, though they too would have a son. I was wearing a dress—I rarely do—and I saw my friend's husband notice me for the first time, saw that I had risen to float above the vision he usually had of me to present something, a certain carefree manner, a casting off of my usual woes, that stood naked with possibility. We had a drink, and went out to dinner and had a few more, and returned to our house and continued drinking. At some point we jumped into the pool wearing our clothes. I yanked my arms out of my dress. The pool was turbulent with bodies, and I was pushed into the deep end where I lost my bearings and went under. When I came back up, my dress slung around my neck, my friend was on the deck, weaving toward the house with a private decisiveness.

The others were toweling off. Inside, I found my friend passed out on the kitchen floor.

The other couple shared a glass of water and drove off. We tried to stop them, didn't we?

The last time I saw my friend was on the Fourth of July. When you have children you feel you must do things, so we took them to a celebration at a park while our husbands remained at home, drinking beer and grilling salmon.

Old people stood around under a tent making pancakes. This wasn't what I wanted to be doing with her. She stood out among all the wandering, fervid, sun-scorched people. Tall and graceful, necklaces slippery with sweat.

Our children slid down a large, inflated waterslide with a couple of hoses running rivulets down the middle. Some friends came over, and I introduced her. I was proud to be in the company of someone so beautiful.

The slide required tickets but no one was collecting them so we let the children go again and again, their skin screeching against the plastic, swim trunks sagging, feet muddy from the two scoops of puddles that had formed at the bottom of the slide. Their joy was so exorbitant it became ours in a way. Finally we left and walked home past the large houses, down the wide street where the parade would soon travel, where low lawn chairs lined the grassy sidewalk strip and you had only embrace what we could not—cheap hope—to the street of smaller houses where my husband and I lived.

THE FUNERAL
MAHREEN
SOHAIL

———

Yesterday I went to my aunt's funeral. She was my father's older sister. Long before he died we lost touch with her and my uncle and their sons. Small misunderstandings arose and then they became bigger until decades had wedged themselves between our families. She had two boys. Every summer, I had begged them to let me play cricket with them. They never said yes, though sometimes they let my brothers play.

At her funeral I saw her two sons again—now men—sitting with bowed heads by her body. From the other guests, I heard that the doctors had said a clot had traveled from her lung all the way to her heart, stopping the flow of blood. Her oldest son was fifty-four now. I had never met his children though I think one of them was the young teenage girl carrying cups of tea back and forth from the kitchen, occasionally bending to receive pats on the back from visiting mourners. My cousins rose to greet me and my mother, and for a second we were all bemused. My mother held my dead aunt's sons—my cousins—and cried. I occasionally sniffed but wasn't able to summon tears. Both cousins had grown up handsome, tall with strong jawlines, their mother's lips trembling on their faces.

I had been told my aunt did not like my mother; that had been the root cause of my father's fight with his sister, and so I examined my mother too, who was small in the room, the corners of her mouth turned down. I wondered if my cousins thought my mother was dramatic as she cried, after all she had not seen them in years. Perhaps she was sad for herself, or sad in the way people are when they realize the end is coming and all the people they have known in their lives are marching in a line towards the edge of the cliff, falling off one by one. The smell of rice cooking wafted through the house. We had also heard that my aunt had been diagnosed with Alzheimer's. During the last two years she had forgotten how to eat, and so there had been a tube in her stomach through which they fed her mush three times a day. She had even forgotten how to talk. Another thing we heard: many years ago when her older son married and brought his wife home, she made the woman stand and pray in the center of the room in her wedding clothes and loudly criticized her form until the new bride burst into tears.

Yesterday, on the way to the funeral, my mother had said, God never forgives some things, and I wondered if she was thinking about this story. But this daughter-in-law, now wedded for many years to the older son, was at the funeral, fine lines around her mouth, holding a boy to her side. Maybe he was seven or eight. Even the woman's mother, the boy's grandmother, was there, and the three of them looked like carbon copies of each other as they spoke in low voices to each other among the other guests.

My aunt's husband, my uncle, was old, almost eighty-seven, and was beginning to forget things too. While I stood in the room trying to pay my condolences to him, another man moved in front of me to say, We are so sorry for your loss, May Allah grant her Jannah.

And my uncle replied, Oh she was so young, only fifty-seven.

The other man said loudly, She was eighty-five. He had the air of a man who was compelled to restore order and I was grateful. I felt afraid suddenly that I would leave here with the number fifty-seven lodged in my brain and later when my mother died, my mind would trick me into comforting myself by thinking, Oh at least she lived longer than my aunt.

No, no, my uncle said. She was fifty-seven.

The other man replied firmly, She was eighty-five.

Finally my uncle looked around the room and, spotting me, asked, Are you eighty-five?

At this my cousins rose from the body's side and said, Abu come with us, and led him out of the room. When we had been kids, the younger one used to eat mayonnaise out of jars because everyone thought it was funny. At meal times whenever we were together, his mother would hand him the jar of mayonnaise after he had eaten his meal and he would open it, dip his finger in, and lick it clean while we all laughed and his mother shook her head as if she did not know what to do with him.

This aunt had not come to the funeral for my father, her own brother. We later heard she was telling people that she had not gone because she knew my mother would not let her in, though she should not have worried—all that day my mother had been preoccupied, glancing at the corners of the living room where we were receiving mourners. My father, in his last days, had started dictating wishes for his burial and the wake. Now she wanted to remember exactly how he'd phrased each wish. She thought the people who had come to pay their respects somehow knew that she was in the process of forgetting. Weeks later she kept asking me, Did so-and-so say anything?

Now my younger cousin came back to where I was standing and spoke to me in a low voice, What are you doing these days? I had heard he was not married. I was surprised to note he had a thin, plaintive voice. I told him I wasn't doing much as if we were old friends, and we were just catching up after a week of not speaking. He nodded, and looked around distracted.

She jumped off the roof, he said.

Startled, I looked over my shoulder as if she had jumped off the roof simply to reappear behind me. She couldn't walk, I reminded him gently, wondering if grief had addled his brain.

She could, he said. He spoke a little louder than he had intended. People turned to look at us. He smiled at my forehead, as if to reassure the room that things were okay. Then he looked directly at me and said, Anyway, what would you know?

She jumped off the roof, I repeated. He nodded, patted my shoulder. It's good to tell someone that, he said. His chin trembled.

In the other room, my uncle was loudly saying to everyone who would listen, I keep telling everyone she was fifty-seven, maybe fifty-eight, and I could hear loud hmms of agreement.

My cousin moved away and I peeked into the room my uncle was speaking in. When my aunt was still alive, someone must have taken care of the couple, reminded him to take his medicine, bathed and fed my aunt when she forgot to do it herself. I saw people exchanging looks as if my aunt had been the one keeping the whole family together and now that she was dead they were witnessing its impending dissolution in real time, *What will happen to this old man now?*

I tried to think of ways to love her. I remembered that when I was a child, we had all been watching TV and she had changed the channel when a commercial for sanitary napkins came on. Then she looked at my mother and said, When we were young, this never would have been on TV, and when I asked her what that meant, she laughed. I imagined her laughing, flying off the roof on a sanitary napkin, yelling, Look how times have changed!

My other cousin, the older one, came up behind me and said, Actually Junaid wasn't feeling that well when he said that. And minds sometimes go where you don't want them to. I couldn't tell if he was talking about his brother's mind or his mother's mind or his own. I looked back to see where my younger cousin was standing in the corner. The two brothers exchanged a look I couldn't decipher.

Of course, I said.

When I thought of my own brothers, who lived far away and were married, I wanted to always love them. Sometimes when they called after weeks of not calling, I picked up the phone anyway to talk to them because I remembered how when my father was dying, you could see in the way his body was becoming just some bones, that he wanted to be held together by people who had known the shape of him as a child.

After my older cousin walked away to greet some guests, Junaid motioned for me to follow him. He led me to the kitchen where a cook was stirring a big spoon into a pot. Chicken? the cook murmured as I passed, and I shook my head. A back door from the kitchen led into the lawn. From there, Junaid and I walked out to the main gate. He walked me all the way around the wall bordering the house until we were facing the back of the house. It was all dirt. He pointed to the ground where you could see a small patch. It looked dark maroon, like it could have been sheep blood, or goat blood, or almost black, like water from sewers had hardened and crusted there. This is where she landed, he said. He looked directly at me. As one, we looked up at the roof. I began to believe it.

I just couldn't take it anymore, he said.

How did she—?

I helped.

You lifted her over the railing?

Yes.

I wondered then if he could kill me too. As if he could read my mind, he quietly said, I just needed someone to know who had known her when she was in her right mind.

I nodded.

He let out a low laugh. I loved her but she could be mean sometimes.

I thought of the jars of mayonnaise and his strained smile as he licked his little fingers clean, and nodded again.

I'm sorry about your father, he said.

He wanted to live, I said. I wanted him to know there was a difference between our parents. When faced with certain death, my father began to celebrate small achievements, like being able to walk on certain days. But still, he had succumbed to death quietly, the only obvious sign of objection the deep, rattling breaths he took on his final day that clanged in my skull for weeks after we buried him. What was the difference between them now that they were both dead?

As if he understood, Junaid nodded, She asked me to do it. She was so sick.

With my foot I scuffed the dirt with my foot, and moved it around. The color began to disappear.

You're okay, I replied, as if saying the words would put him back together. I remembered then that I had said those words to my father when he was in the hospital and needed blood drawn, needed a new test, got some bad news.

I realized now that I missed saying those words, that I wanted to repeat them forever to everyone I had ever known. I was afraid I would grow old and not know anyone willing to say them back to me.

Yes, he replied, I'm okay. Can I call you sometimes?

Before I could agree, we began to hear people calling his name in the house so we made our way back inside. His older brother glared at us as we entered.

The men picked up the body to carry it outside and eventually to the graveyard. Junaid started to make a loud keening sound as soon as they lifted her. She jumped, he said loudly. She really, really jumped. I helped her, he said. I dropped her in one go. Everyone shushed him as they carried the body out the door. You could tell they wanted to bury her quickly, smooth the earth over this whole day so everyone could go back to their routines. Under the ground there was my father and soon my aunt and one day it would be this son, who was wailing loudly as he got into the ambulance with the body, I pulled the tube out of her stomach and lifted her! Everyone shook their heads. Those boys really loved their mother, I heard a woman whisper to another woman.

After the men took my aunt's body to the graveyard, I finally went and sat in the big lounge where all the women were sitting. My mother was already there and she made space for me next to her and for just one moment I felt like I had when I was a child and wanted to be near her all the time. I looked around the room, at all the people and distant relatives my aunt had collected in her lifetime. It surprised me that she had continued to deserve and receive generosity from people even during all those years we were estranged. These people would not come to my mother's funeral. My father used to say, The point of life is to collect people to come to your funeral.

There was an older woman there and she was snoring on the sofa. I took off my shoes and put my handbag to the side. My mother and I began to read from the Quran. My aunt's grandchildren came in and out of the room, and the women spoke in low voices about their daily lives. Some of them knew my name even though I had never seen them before. They said, How are you? Good, I replied.

Suddenly I was very exhausted. Like the old woman on the sofa, I just wanted to sleep. The men began to come back. They looked tired, and their shoes were caked in dust from where they had stood around the grave when my aunt's body was lowered into it. Junaid was quiet now. He came in and went straight upstairs to his room. I knew then that I would never see him again.

Every year, my aunt's family had visited or we had visited them during the long summer holidays in June, July, and August. My brothers and our two cousins and I had spent the days jostling for space on a sofa while playing Nintendo, only stopping to break for food. For dessert we kept blocks of ice cream in the freezer. They came packaged in long rectangles of cardboard. If we left the ice cream sitting out too long, it would begin to leak out of the cardboard's edges. My mother would bring an ice cream block out after every meal, and all of us would watch as she quickly use a knife to cut the smooth rectangle into even pieces for us. We held out our bowls where she dropped our share in. After that, my father and my aunt would begin to argue about what would go best with the ice cream and for a few moments, the rest of us had a feeling that they had forgotten us. Cornflakes, coconut shavings, packets of crisps, french fries. They would put something different into every bowl, and then we would pass them around the table so everyone could vote on what tasted the best. Usually my aunt's choices of what went best with ice cream won, and then she would beam for the rest of the night. Now I think my father let her win. It was a wonderful thing when she smiled. There are many things we take to our graves just because there is no language for how to recount the experience of having lived through them.

Finally my mother motioned for me to get up; it was time for us to go home. From the window, I could see it was a new moon that night, a lovely spring evening. I moved my foot absently as if to find my shoe. It touched leather and I looked down and saw I had put my foot into my handbag. I glanced around quickly to make sure that no one was watching, but the old woman was awake now and she was watching. What an idiot, she said loudly, and then she began to laugh. It took only a second for everyone to see what she was laughing at, and then suddenly the room was alight with laughter. I was prepared to feel hurt but it felt gentle and edifying; that whole evening I had felt like I was walking on something fragile and finally that thing had broken, and now my mother and I were falling through air. All our relatives, all these people we had not seen for years, held us aloft for a bit as they must have done when my parents were younger and when I was a child, and then finally the laughter died, and we were on our way.

GHOST IN TRANSLATION
MARZIA GRILLO

——

JULY I

Dear Sara,

Let's pretend you never said Get out of my life and we still write to each other like we used to. The war is over but we never—not even from a distance—thought about rebuilding. But literature is predictable. The structuring of a narrative has its highs and lows, cycles and countercycles that lead to a happy ending. You wanted to disappear in India and instead you're in Liguria. I'm almost forty and you're immortal. Don't you think we've grown up enough? We survived ourselves.

g.

JULY 4

Dear S.,

I won't ask what happened these past seven years. Where you've been, who did what, if you were forced to come back to Italy or decided for yourself. I won't keep asking. It won't get to the point where you think that you've already told me, and that I understood it all, and that the world is simpler than it is. I'll be still and quiet, I'll listen to what you're ready to tell me, if you want to. This is what nice people do.

Anyway.

g.

JULY 7

Dear S.,

We met when we worked together, and then at a certain point you stopped working with everyone I was in touch with, you cut off contact. You became a taboo subject: Have you heard from her? Shrug. And you? Not us..

Now you have reappeared, we—the two of us—are working together again, and I can tell you that it's at once terrifying and magnificent.

You translate novels, and I revise them. You have a rare talent and this is why your work creates sparks, a fuse between authorship and service. I insert apostrophes and straighten out meanings, but you make everything better. No one has ever said that miracles occur, that books change, in good translations of bad literature. Then what's the point of these crusades? Self-love? Flirtation? Altruism?

It would be great if publishing was just work. It would be great if you were just you and that was that, and I was less than zero, like in the eighties.

g.

JULY 9

Dear Sara,

Remember when in 2010 I put your name in an appendix? A tribute, a bouquet of letters.

That spring, we said good-bye on a train platform in Bologna. I was coming home from a wedding, where my father spoke about me to an acquaintance and thought I wasn't listening. He said he was worried about his daughter because she'd never gotten over the death of her mother, it was as if she was plagued by it. That was the first time I saw myself from the outside in, and it frightened me. I left without saying good-bye, got off at Bologna and asked you to meet me there. You know the rest.

g.

JULY 11

Dear S.,

This morning our publisher forwarded me a complaint from a reader. He was vicious, listing typos I'd left in our book. I checked, and they were all there. Christ, he'd even marked the double spaces! There were some translation errors on his list too, and those are partly yours. Essentially, according to him, we'd totally distorted and betrayed the story's spirit.

Here's a man who knows what betrayal is, I thought.

g.

PS: Speaking of betrayal and interpretation: even with all the experience you have, can you ever fully be sure when you decide to translate with *bye* instead of *see you*?

JULY 15

Dear S.,

This morning the sky fell onto the city, a series of brief storms punctuated by lightning: the summer downpours of your concise sentences. When it doesn't rain for ages and then comes all at once, even our world holds its breath. It doesn't help to live somewhere full of disparity, like India, or of surprises, like Thailand.

With those haywire clouds and windows open wide to the tumult, it occurred to me that you've come back so alive that our lives seem aligned. Now you no longer write me letters, and rarely email. Instead, you send me voice memos on WhatsApp about when you can or can't work on a text. You no longer tie each word with string and I can hear background noise—I never listen to your messages twice—but anyway it's nice you're there. It's nice India didn't make you vanish. You changed horizons, and now your Instagram photos are from all over the world but I know you're nearby, with a time difference that's bearable. With emails that don't bounce back automatically.

g.

Dear S.,

You made me believe your universe was immense. Not just because you knew more languages, but because you could cut me out of your life and survive. What's the solar system compared to galaxies? I'd raise my eyes to the sky and not find you. But when you stopped looking around and returned to point A, I was fixed at the same spot, waiting for you.

Let's face it: for a long time, your universe was vaster than mine. You created chaos and I lingered to remember, to ask myself unanswerable questions.

g.

Dear Sara,

I never told you about the time I fell in love with C. It was terrifying, but it doesn't exist for you because you were gone for so many years. There's this gigantic ellipsis in our shared history, there's our late youth frozen and taken up again after everything that's happened, and now I feel sort of foreign with you.

Are we false friends?

g.

Dear Sara,

Sometimes I think you're a ghost.

We only saw each other in person twice, but we wrote hundreds of emails and messages.

Perhaps that's why, despite your good-bye, I was prepared to see you come back. It's the thing about you I was most familiar with: your delays, your breaks, the fine-print flaws in your punctuation, your regionalisms. In some way I knew you'd leave the subject blank in your next email, to bridge the time in our distance.

Actually, an instant was enough to stop time.

g.

AUGUST 2

Dear S.,

Once I told you that after my mother died I started seeing a spirit in my room. I couldn't banish it so I called it Holy (never give names to ghosts, a friend once scolded, unless you want to adopt them).

Years apart, you disappeared too, and your absence became matter in the same way. I told myself at least I'd learned something: it's good to keep some disappearances alive. So I started dressing this new ghost in your colors: a bright-red sari, gold at the neck, flat leather shoes. It used to walk next to me, it inhabited all my houses (the ones you've never seen), it visited countries and cities you've never been to. I've called to it in so many ways, but it hasn't answered me yet.

g.

AUGUST 8

Dear S.,

In the past, we sent each other small treasures: photos, newspaper clippings, coins, matchbooks, sugar packets, origami, books with underlined passages that, if arranged in a row, formed little stories within the larger narratives. Despite our distance, we appropriated places, time, light. Often, these novels were about terrible, thoughtless love. I wanted to exorcize it—you celebrated it. Not long ago, I picked up the last book you sent me, the one where you'd underlined the line "to live love as despair," and right after: "to escape everywhere, criminal-like."

g.

AUGUST 16

Dear S.,

 I opened a dictionary and looked up *betrayal*, and there were many more synonyms than antonyms. Then I looked up *loyalty*, which also had more synonyms. How could this be?

g.

AUGUST 28

Dear S.,

I've been thinking again about the leaf cigarettes you used to send me from

India when we first met, and about my past lovers' gold-and-pastel Sobranies (similarly foreign), and I can't make peace with my straight-cut tobacco and this evening's Bombay and sparkling water. Where have we ended up? Did you really come back to Italy? It doesn't seem like you did. Perhaps you're in France, Aotearoa, or Cuba. Perhaps you lost your meaning in translation, and it's not up to me to find it.

g.

SEPTEMBER 2

Dear S.,

Last night I dreamed that C. found the key to Simenon's success by studying combinations of words according to their length. I looked at her admiringly, I thought: It's so simple, so straightforward, to write a perfect novel—until I understood that C. had analyzed the Italian translation and not the original. Does it still count?

And you: Do you still count?

g.

SEPTEMBER 9

Dear S.,

When we met we wrote to each other continually, I could scarcely keep up with the pace of our enthusiasm. You were omnipresent, omnivorous, omnipotent, like jellyfish. You stitched tigers.

I sent you photos from Florence, Venice, Rome—I answered when I was entirely myself and also often when I was entirely elsewhere.

Then one time I told you that from backgammon I'd learned to cheat and you started responding to me differently, until you ended everything.

Maybe I broke something with the backgammon story? Did I become for you, from that moment, an unreliable narrator?

Anyway, I spent the years you were absent discovering and cultivating the so-called truth of narrative, where whoever is writing dictates the rules. It's something that relaxes me. Now I no longer need to play backgammon because cheating does nothing for me: I revise the rules whenever I want, I decide what is real and what isn't.

I'll get to the point, S.: it's time to choose whether you want to be part of this private universe. You can leave, if you prefer. I can delete you from my rules, if it's what you really want. Then we'd truly lose each other, not like in the past.

g.

SEPTEMBER 10

Dear S.,
I wasn't being serious when I talked about our chances of losing each other. Is it because you took me literally, to the letter, that you stopped responding to me?

g.

SEPTEMBER 12

Dear S.,
…

SEPTEMBER 25

Dear Sara,
You probably won't read these last lines of mine, but today something incredible happened, and I can't keep it to myself: your ghost started to speak!

This morning it uttered its first word in a language I'd never heard before in my life. It sounded strange, the voice of a Machine: mechanical yet at the same time ancient. The rest of the day, your ghost stayed quiet, indifferent.

I tried to reassure it, said that we always have to start somewhere, that each word—irrationally—has more synonyms than antonyms, etcetera.

And as for us: thank you for being there.

g.

SOLITUDES.COM

ALLISON TITUS

I have to confess   I thought it would be different

this time   I mean all of it

abbreviated sun snap   through the window

of the new house   blurred-out powerline sky

the flick-feather mockingbird   that swoops after

me & my dog   in the yard

Fig trees   & privacy fences   FedEx trucks

full of perishables & new denim

I'm sure   I thought   I was on to something

brand-new   & life-affirming

as ever in pursuit   of the better version & its full

potential   which continues, as ever, to elude me—

but all I felt for months was a hazy form of dread

so like a veil I wore it   until the next

season begins   is brighter

& I'm getting to the end   of The Loneliness Scale

A test invented in California where I cried in a hotel

pool at daybreak under the palm trees

once now look at me, taking inventory

by rating the distance between the Day-Glo & the atmospheric

like the volta in the final hour

as the newest fantasy takes it up a notch.

It would be boring to tell you the truth

which is: I fell in love & everything changed

overnight & suddenly it happened to me like walking without

looking

straight into a tree the crepe myrtle branch slung low & sloppy

with blossoms in that gauzy morning sunlight

in the new backyard & the flowers exploded

getting everywhere —snagging my hair, the air, the too-

tall grass—

petals spinning into the summer breeze like confetti

in a minor parade. All over me.

Luigi Ghirri

OF THE DISTEMPERS OF HORSES

ROBERT OSTROM

It was easy to deceive for the season
of the year was spring and even
the circumspect stood at their windows
employing gestures that looked more
like reaching than pointing at hyacinths
white and pink, camellia red, yellowthroats
in yellow weeds on the seedbare
ground. Waiting for news can make
a neighborhood come apart: first
an eaves trough unhinges then a busted
watermain then divorce. The roorback
says your life doesn't matter. Did you think
this was going to be something to post
on your wall, a wreath to hang on your
door. This is what keeps you up at night:
sensible dread stored in the granary
of your cells. How does it feel to feel
them inside, clambering up ladders,
pulling drop pins on the old gates, your
ancestors who knew how to husband
wisely. The mud wind cold when the
shutters bust open. They who survived
countless shocks that flesh is heir to,
as many lives as there are hooks
to stretch the fabric of you. They must
tremble at the thought that all of this is
because your problems are the problems
of sheep. Even a herdbound horse
sick with the strangles will mettle up,
ears pinned, eyes rolled to the whites.
It falls back, stands alone and fights.

Luigi Ghirri

ON FIRST LOOKING INTO EMILY WILSON'S HOMER

CECILY PARKS

Each summer I swim in a lake that the sun turns gold
Toward sister islands piled high with pines
As if I were a homegoing heroine
Whom gods had spelled from becoming ugly or old.
Water-going women are not, I've been told,
As epically interesting as goddesses, monsters, or sirens;
Yet after Homer's princess washes garments,
She saves a hero whom Wilson never describes as bold.
Knowing this is like reaching the distant rise
Of a new shore, having swum faster than
A wooden boat helmed by a war-wise
King, but actually it's the moment when
Penelope says, "I am the prize"
That I continue to take most pleasure in.

Luigi Ghirri

THE LAMP OF DRAMA

JOSHUA EDWARDS

Out of the solar myth a play
emerged about a holy place
where the shadow of a temple
was cast across adjacent graves
for just one autumn hour, to give
two phantoms a brief reunion.

Staged mainly for nobility
at first, it later came to be
allegory for social themes.
The lovers took three centuries
to change their clothes. With time, the robes
they wore as gentry would be rags.

What was said and how it was said
also changed as the years went by,
as the rules of society
were transformed into suggestions,
and meanings once held in gesture
became the property of speech.

Always the audience remained
hungry for, more than anything,
the sound of that couple talking
beyond worldly recognition.
It really didn't matter what
they said, as long as they were dead.

Luigi Ghirri

FICTION / MARK HAGE

ROME, NEW YORK

He immigrated not long ago, and he is walking through the big blizzard. He did not fully understand snow and cold, never came across the Rule of Threes. Three minutes without breath, three days without water, three hours outside without a proper coat. There were no buses, and he thought he could walk to the shared apartment after his last delivery. He had been through his first month of winter, and his jacket and loafers were fine, adequate. He thought it was in jest that people suggested heavier clothing, and laughed as if he understood the joke. He knew within a few minutes this was different. He felt a sensation in his body that at first was opposable, amusing, refutable with a smile and gritted teeth. But then creeping, it became overpowering, inexorable; a sudden raised volume. He had read *Tintin* as a kid, Tintin was also in Tibet, near a summit. He could remember Tintin walking in the snow with his dog, Milou. His pants tucked in his socks, a blue hooded sweatshirt jacket just like his; his feet never sinking more than a light dent.

He knocked on the first door he saw, he knew enough now to realize another three miles won't do. He saw someone peer out and let the curtain go. He waited. The porch gave him a reprieve from the vertical component of what was racing down, sourced from places he could not see. The horizontal battering was still ongoing, harder it seemed in its isolated direction; full of what felt like pebbles wet and hard, making different sounds against his face and clothes, a different thumping against his wet shoes. It felt like a drumming with a thousand fingers. He was colder now, and somehow he knew that he was still fine as long as he felt colder, felt anything. His toes was where the pain started. His gloved hands were also starting to feel a pain, but a different one. He knew severe weather of the opposite kind: warm, humid, scorching, but he never thought that could kill.

Froze to death. He had heard that somewhere. He thought it was an American figure of speech, those exaggerations he had to sort out from the teachings he got in English from an international volume called *First Things First. Froze to death, I can eat a horse*. Who can eat a horse? He had laughed. He knocked again, and the curtains stayed shut. He walked out from under the porch, his feet were imprinting a pattern, his geometry into a perpetually renewing whiteness, soon unblemished, mesmerizing. He stopped for a second and looked back at what he had done and marveled at the loveliness of it. He had made the same pattern as a kid and wished he could import that one from so long ago, put it side by side with these fresh ones. Umber and white, clay and snow, to see how different his stride was now, how much he grew. He pushed through the strengthening wind and saw a woman in a car. How lucky she was, he thought. He stood looking at her. She looked back at him. He did not ask to join her, a car is intimate, no room to allow for the polite separation he needed with a stranger, a woman. He walked on, saw a house with an American flag and the top of a red sign stuck in the yard. He kept walking, sinking deeper, starting to feel less, getting used to the pain and its strange bearable constance.

He understood so much more. Everything people talked about. Things he thought meant one thing but now clear to mean something different. In a way he understood everything. All that was ever said to him, and whatever had come to his mind. It all fell into place. It was now nearly complete.

FICTION

ERRATICS
KATE
WALBERT
—

She noticed the cardinal often—red, male—in the months after her father died, October 1993, when it seemed she noticed everything, or nothing, meaning things would slip into her view and then out of her view, as if the ship on which she stood—its bow, or stern, she never remembered which— was moving at an interminable speed, and the things of the world were stationary, just out of reach, and she wasn't interested in them anyway. The things of the world? she heard her father say. Drop the bullshit. What did she mean by *things*, or, *the world*, but he was dead and so the question remained, *remains*, unasked, or asked in the way of her father now, everywhere and nowhere.

The cardinal, bright red, brilliant red, perched most mornings on the railing of what her landlady called her back deck, though Grace would call it a stoop, just a landing off the stairway up to her back door; a stairway to a stoop she never much used, anyway. She was an inside kind of person, especially now, here, in these woods, and so she's mostly used the stoop for storage—a hammock chair she couldn't figure out how to secure to the ceiling, a dead houseplant (one of the four Max gave her for good luck, and better air quality), and the half-empty paint can and stiff brushes from an aborted attempt to brighten the living room—she'd stopped at one wall, either from ennui or laziness, she couldn't tell which, and besides, the lime green that had looked so plucky in the magazine looked lousy here, her walls resisted, she'd told Max, her best friend back in New York. They literally revolted, she said. They were roiling with anger. They were like, totally pissed off.

Were you high? Max said.

Maybe, she said.

The apartment was on the top floor of a complicated house, not exactly early Victorian, but definitely not mid-century modern, more twentieth-century aspirational, with bay windows off the second-floor bedrooms—nice—and a converted patio with jalousie windows—not so nice. On the tour, her landlady, Mrs. Simpson, had pointed out the oak paneling of a rec room in the basement—converted, she said, for her husband and her son, Scott, now grown and living on his own closer to town but on Sundays when the college games were on, well. Boys! Scott worked as a handyman for "the property," by which Mrs. Simpson meant the third-floor apartment she rented on a month-to-month basis. They would get to that in a minute, Mrs. Simpson had said, standing off the foyer within the jungle of the wallpapered powder room. First, she wanted to take the temperature of the inquirer.

In a different story, Mrs. Simpson might have worn a housecoat, something faintly glamorous, perhaps polka-dotted, smoke curling from the cigarette, a Virginia Slim, she kept balanced on her bottom lip except to occasionally ash in the orange plastic ashtray she carried with nicotine-yellowed fingers, her teeth best left unmentioned. But the truth is, Mrs. Simpson was in a tennis skirt, opening cupboards to replace a glass or find the mug for the tea she offered—yes, thank you—straightening hand towels as Grace assured her she was fine with temperature taking, in fact more than fine, and her temperature was steady as she goes, her temperature was reliable with a capital R. A double R. Responsible, too. Her temperature was Responsible. And Neat. And Quiet as a mouse, never so quiet, *looking* for quiet.

Mrs. Simpson shrugged. That's fine, she said. No one else seems interested.

The house sat at the end of a road, a very long dirt road that dead-ended against a bank of white pine and spruce, birch, too, spindly and dwarfed by the evergreens, like some tall, lanky cousins who disappear in the family portrait. Mrs. Simpson had said that in the spring, their light green leaves were stunning against the black of the forest.

Sweet, she hears her father say.

I'm too young to have a dead father, she says back to him.

This was January, and now it is late March, and Grace is beginning to see a little of what Mrs. Simpson meant, the bright green, yellowish birch leaf fans of color against the black spruce, evergreen and dark pine, the endlessness of it there, where she hasn't hiked though she'd been encouraged—something about an erratic a mile or so in, a thing to hike to, a thing to see: the way the stone balanced on the ledge, as if intentional, though pushed a million years ago by the glaciers that formed the Blue Ridge Mountains, or the Rocky Mountains, or some mountain range somewhere near here: Asheville, she said to herself and not for the first time. I'm in Asheville, North Carolina.

That the red cardinal is her father, Grace is entirely sure. Of other things, not so much.

She took the job as a nanny as a lark and besides, she's never really been qualified for anything: a Masters in Existential Prose, a degree the university made up in order to rope in people at loose ends, her father had said. I would call that, he said, a Masters in Loose Ends.

Exactly, she said. Existential.

Sartrah for Dummies, he said. He of the New York City doctors. The Weill Cornell and New York-Presbyterian set. He of the story of dining with Cole

Porter—or was it Oscar Hammerstein?—at a Westchester party hosted by a principal dancer from the New York City Ballet, or something, a flat tire involved. A fifth of gin. This in the fifties—could it have been the fifties?—before she was born, when a flat tire was a thing. Not just a call to Triple A, her father said.

Still, Asheville?

Fresh air, she said. The smell of pines. The Black Mountain School. Rauschenberg and also, the guy who invented the geodesic dome.

Buckminster Fuller, he'd said.

Right, him, she said. No Oscar Hammerstein, she'd said (it *was* Oscar Hammerstein, she remembered), but close enough.

He'd smiled then, her father, and she loved him so much she can't bear to think about it now. The smile. And how he'd shrugged and said, It's your funeral.

Or is it the female who is red?

Are you my fuckin' mother? she called out, remembering the terrifying book, palm size, she reads to the little girl in her charge: Missy. An old-fashioned name that fits her, Suzanne, her mother, had explained, like a glove, as if she should apologize for her daughter's name, and her daughter's ways: Missy a child who prefers to sit and push a needle through cloth, stitching her initials on her socks, on her underpants, on the sleeves of her long-sleeved T-shirts as if she's anticipating summer camp in her future and wants to save Suzanne the trouble, which, in truth, is rather kind: Suzanne a very busy woman and Missy's father no longer in the picture, nor a person to be discussed, *entre nous*.

Is that French? her father had asked.

Ha ha, she said. She had told him her plan: move to Asheville at the beginning of the new year, get her shit together, babysit, write a novel, or at least the outline of one.

An existential outline? he'd said.

They sat in their New York kitchen around the white, oval table—decidedly seventies—eating Chinese.

"I thought it might be a good plan," she had said.

"Well, it's a plan," he'd said.

What had she ordered? Szechuan beef with broccoli. Sesame noodles (his favorite). Wonton soup. Dumplings, pork. She had never had to ask for his order; she knew him by heart.

He twirls a noodle on his chopstick and pops it into his mouth.

"I've never been south of the Mason-Dixon line," he says.

Behind him, through the kitchen window, the Winstons in 5F appear to be eating Chinese as well. White cartons on their kitchen table, a stiff brown paper bag. Perhaps everyone in the entire city is eating Chinese, Grace thinks; it's that kind of day.

"We went to Florida that time," she says.

"Oh God, right. Florida," her father says. "So unfortunate. You got that terrible sunburn."

"Baby oil and iodine," she says.

"And your mother had a headache for six days."

"Typical," she says, spearing a dumpling. The grease tastes good in her mouth though it burns her tongue.

"And when we finally got back to Seventy-Third street, she knelt on the sidewalk and wept," her father says.

"She did not."

"Oh, right," he says. "That was me."

"Mom wouldn't want to dirty her knees," she says.

"She had lovely knees."

"Is that Salinger?" she says.

"No," he says. "Your mother," he says. They were almost finished with it. The meal. The kitchen. Their lives together. A few years earlier, Grace's mother, her father's ex-wife, Paulette, had left him, had left them, for a film director in Los Angeles. This kitchen. This table. The Winstons in 5F. Ever since everything had seemed anachronistic, as if Grace and her father were slowly burning out, or suffocating, the two of them finishing a story in an already closed book. And Paulette, thousands of miles away, couldn't have cared less. She only dropped a line from time to time, sometimes writing *miss you* but never, ever *wish you were here.*

Scott, the son, the handyman, tromps up the back stairs. It has begun to snow, big icy flakes, wet as rain on Scott's shoulders, or his jacket, one of the kind usually associated with hunting. Was Scott a hunter? She had never before noticed his eyes.

And her still in her stocking feet and PJs.

"Sorry, didn't Mom tell you?" he says.

"What?"

"Your stove. I thought she'd told you."

"Oh," Grace says. "Right," she says. "I think she did," she says. "There's a problem."

"I know," he says.

They both stand as if waiting for something.

"It's snowing," he says.

"It is," she says. *Stupid.*

"Can I come in?"

The cardinal flits up to the spruce, she sees and, yes, flits, darting here and there as if it thinks it's a chickadee, or a sparrow, or one of those other types of birds without the wherewithal to glide, or soar.

"Grace?"

"Oh yeah," she says. "Sorry. Man! It's freezing!"

He's stomping his boots—boots!—on the doormat she put at the back door for eventual visitors. She had inherited it from her father or rather, she took it from the apartment. He of the Oscar Hammerstein set, the great doctor, hadn't left her any instruction, unless you counted the handwritten note on the index card above the kitchen sink, its fading ink a directive in his steady, surgeon's hand: *Old building, Old pipes, Let the Water Run Clear.* But then again, he had died in an instant: a major cardiac event. The shoemaker's shoes, etc.

The doormat reads: *Ask Not for Whom the Dog Barks. It Barks for Thee.*

"Funny," Scott says.

"It was funnier when I had a dog," she says. In truth, they never had a dog. Her father had just found the doormat funny, like Paulette found the needlepoint pillow someone had stitched with *A Woman needs a Man like a Fish needs a Bicycle* funny. It was the sixties, she would say. You have no idea.

Scott hangs his coat on her coatrack, also her father's though Grace supposes now hers, one of the many objects she had loaded with Max's help into a U-Haul she'd rented for thirty dollars a day and mileage—deceptive!!—and driven, alone, down West End and over the GW Bridge thinking, Shit, shit, shit, what am I doing? Thinking, shit, shit, shit, New Jersey! Also in her U-Haul: the round coffee table her father had refinished, its legs turned on a wood lathe—those gams are lithe, he had said; the useless cigar boxes he collected, each with its own useless contents; a trombone he played in the army marching band, long story, though his uniform was there too, packed in the trunk he took to Columbia University, and then to Korea. Nothing to tell, he would say. It was the fifties, he'd say. Great fun.

You are the most obstinate man in the world, she would have told him, had she been with him when he died. But she was not. She was crosstown, at the cinema, or what he called the cinema—is that French? she'd ask—and though she would like to say that something had shifted for her in that moment, sitting in a gummy seat in front of the huge screen, watching the huge faces of the actors, an interruption, or a chill, a dropped heartbeat twinned with his, or better, the weight of her father's hand on her shoulder, his beautiful surgeon's hand with its calluses and pared nails, its soapy smell, nothing happened of the sort. Nothing happened at all.

"Here's the little fucker," Scott says. He's already jimmied the stove from the back wall. The day's gone gray, or snowy. Snowy gray, the cardinal no longer in view; perhaps hiding, or perhaps it soared away. No matter. Scott shows her the frayed wire as if it were a splinter he's just extracted, or a fish hook.

This is what Grace knows of cardinals. They seem to fancy northern reaches, but have been seen as far south as Louisiana. They enjoy larger seeds, sunflower, pumpkin. They mate for life—no, she made that up: no one knows how long a cardinal mates, but definitely not for life. Never for life. Cardinals are randy, she suspects. They get around like most birds: little fuckers.

"Ha," Scott says.

He sits across from her in her father's favorite reading chair, drinking the coffee she prepared for him on her newly working stove, boiling the water in a soup pot—she hadn't yet gotten around to anything fancier—his legs crossed, his boots still on. Has she mentioned his eyes?

"That's the thing," she says. "People don't know. People don't even notice most birds, and they're like everywhere."

"You mean cardinals?" Scott says.

"Birds," she says.

Could she be any clearer? "I mean birds in general," she says. "You know, robins. Chickadees. Sparrows."

"Mockingbirds," Scott says.

"Mockingbirds," she says.

"We've got lots of those, too," Scott says.

"Exactly," she says. She takes a sip of her coffee though it's gone cold. "Those are the worst little fuckers," Scott says. "They'll fucking steal the eggs from another bird's nest."

"Really?" she says. "I thought those were cowbirds."

"Oh right," Scott says. "Cowbirds."

"Anyway," she says. "Nobody notices birds is the thing. And someday, there won't be any left. And no one will notice because no one noticed in the first place. No one ever paid enough attention."

"To birds?" Scott says. Still, those eyes. She takes another cold sip of coffee.

"Yes," she says. "Birds."

She could eat Scott for breakfast, and maybe she will. Wash him down with cold coffee. He's the first man she's touched in a thousand years.

She looks out to her view of the spruce, the white pine, the boughs now heavy with wet snow—no one needs to tell her it will all be gone in hours, the snow a fluke, she understands, and everyone concerned for safety. Suzanne had left a message on her answering machine: STAY HOME!!!! TOO DANGEROUS!!!!

"Happy to service you anytime, ma'am," Scott says, behind her. *Really?*

"What's the charge, sir," she says.

"No charge, ma'am."

He hugs her, his chin on her shoulder.

"I like you," he says.

Somewhere, out there, her father, still brilliant, still red, plucks a nit from his gorgeous feathers, smooths the down of his breast, flexes his scaly, dinosaur bird claws against the scratch of the bark, holding on. He's got a mate somewhere, but she's flown the coop. It doesn't matter; she's far less beautiful than he, her feathers a dull brown, leaden even, her concern primarily the nest—*boring*—the bigger the better, she tells him; this new nest of hers, she says, is spun from gold, lined with copper pennies that catch the sun, hold the heat. She's traded up and out, she tells him.

Grace watches the snow weigh down the spruce bough; with any gust of wind it could snap. *Come back little fucker,* she thinks.

Scott pulls her tighter. "What are you thinking?" he says.

"Missy," she says. "I was thinking of Missy. The kid I babysit," she says. "I was thinking how much fun she must be having in the snow."

"Ten-four," Scott says. "Snow's the best when you're a kid."

Across town, Missy was having no fun at all, mainly because her mother was having no fun at all, despite it being one of the rare days when both Missy and Suzanne were home from their responsibilities: at kindergarten (Missy felt especially responsible at kindergarten—for what, she wasn't sure. It was just a sharp feeling that gave her a stomachache), and the shop (Suzanne ran a floral boutique in town, Peach Blossoms). In fact, not only was Suzanne having no fun at all, she was panicking: an important delivery of freesias and calla lilies were trapped by a jack-knifed tractor trailer on Highway 70, presumably ruined.

"*Maman,*" Missy says—she's enrolled in a bilingual kindergarten, very selective—"You *said.*"

"I did say," Suzanne says. What she said she's not entirely sure, though she imagines it has something to do with plastic fruit and a miniature shopping cart, primary colored, Missy received several months ago from Santa, her favorite game ever since involving tiny slips of paper she Scotch tapes with prices to the plastic tomato, lemon, and avocado, Velcroed so they can be sliced in half with the plastic knife on the plastic cutting board and then immediately resurrected to play the game, again. And again.

"I'd like three pounds of tomatoes please," Suzanne says. "I'm making a Bolognese and I'm fresh out."

"Three pounds," Missy says, squinting as if she's conjuring the price in the far distance. Suzanne notices the fading freckles on her daughter's nose and pokes them one, two, three.

"Ouch," Missy says.

"You're just so damn cute," Suzanne says.

"*Merci,*" Missy says.

"You're welcome," Suzanne says.

Missy hands her a string bag with a single tomato.

"I lost the other one," she says.

Since the Christmas grocery-cart purchase, Suzanne has bought Missy additional plastic fruit, armloads of plastic fruit, and an apron, a small wooden spoon and whisk, and a red cash register that dings.

"*Mon Dieu!* A weak Bolognese, oh well," Suzanne says, dropping the string bag with the tomato into the miniature shopping cart. "Monsieur will be displeased but he is always displeased. *Mon Dieu!* Monsieur is a difficult man."

Missy squints into the distance.

"Would you like to buy a lemon?" she asks.

"Okay," Suzanne says.

"Two quarters," Missy says, holding out her little palm.

"Highway robbery!" Suzanne says, and Missy begins to cry.

"What is it about cardinals and fathers?" Max says. "My friend Cathy's father came back as a cardinal, too."

"Shut up," Grace says.

"True story," Max says.

Grace sits in her father's favorite reading chair, listening, winding and unwinding the curly cord to the receiver; she had actually called to tell Max about Scott, though there wasn't much to tell in the end.

"That's what she said," Max says.

"Who?" Grace says.

"Cathy," Max says. He's in the tiny studio he rents in Hell's Kitchen—a steal—working on his own novel, though the windows must be opened—overheated! Jesus!—so the sound of Max is the sound of the traffic of Tenth Avenue, the delivery trucks and the taxis and the assholes, Max says, who seem to intentionally aim to run him down any time he attempts to cross the street to the bodega on Fifty-First, which he does more than he cares to admit, given the slow progress of his novel, and the guys who man the counter.

"Who?" Grace says.

"Cathy!" Max yells. "She told me she'd be washing dishes and the cardinal wouldn't leave her alone—he'd tap on the window as if he had some important message to deliver—tap, tap, tap. Tap, tap, tap—it drove her nuts."

"She didn't listen to him?" Grace says.

"What?" Max yells.

"Never mind," Grace says.

"It finally went away," Max yells. "That's what Cathy said. Flew south for the winter or something."

"That's geese," Grace says.

"Yeah, well, maybe cardinals too, what do I know?" Max says.

She hears what sounds like a wind tunnel, that edgy whistle, grating. "Goddamn truckers," Max says.

"Little fuckers," she says.

"The point is," Max says, suddenly quieter, and sharper—he's closed the window. "The point is, Cathy's father flew away—I guess they do. I mean it seems fathers stop in to say hello, to maybe hang out for a while, but then they're gone, Grace. That's the point. They're gone."

Why Missy is inconsolable Suzanne has no idea, though she's been holding her daughter on her lap for what feels like hours as the little girls shoulders shake, as she cries and cries and cries, the tears wetting the knees of her big girl tights, tights she has insisted on putting on this morning despite her mother's good news that it's a snow day, and so there will be no school, and there will be no Grace, and the two of them will—how fun!—spend the whole day together, comfy and warm, and so she could stay in her pjs and have as many slices of cinnamon toast for breakfast as she would like, because no one is rushing around this morning, there is no train to catch.

"Where are we going?" Missy had asked.

"What do you mean?" Suzanne had said. "Nowhere!"

"On the train?" Missy said.

"Nowhere!" Suzanne said. She squatted next to her daughter's big-girl bed, and her legs felt creaky.

"To nowhere?" her daughter asked, and Suzanne, legs stiff, stiff and creaky—the barometric pressure!—had stretched into downward dog and entirely forgotten the question. And now Missy cries and cries because, if she could say it, the snake—Grace has told her this is what makes her stomach hurt, it's a snake that coils so tight there, waiting to strike, and that the best thing to do with a snake like that is to pretend it's something else, to pretend it's a kitten, or a soft baby bunny that just wants to be safe and warm and keep to itself in the dark, if you just think of these other things then the snake will eventually get bored, Grace said, and slither out—how? Missy asked, but Grace just shook her head. Snakes have their ways, she said. It's a mystery.

"Gross," Missy said.

"Not like that!" Grace said, and they laughed and laughed, but Grace had not told the truth because Missy's tummy still hurt, it ached and ached, the snake wrapped so tight she could feel it, and no room to breathe, or to eat any more of her cinnamon toast, or to stop her crying, she must stop her crying this instant, her mother says. How can she be crying when it is a snow day? A lovely snow day? Look at all the snow! her mother is saying. Look! And it is true, the snow is so pretty, and the cold of the window feels good against her hot face, the glass there, and if she breathes in a certain way, the glass fogs and she can write her initials, *MP*, that she's been practicing so carefully in school for Mademoiselle Bolduc, her pretty teacher with the beautiful black shoes she polishes while the others sleep for nap but not her, not Missy, because that's when the snake in her tummy feels the worst, something she has only told Grace, her pretty babysitter, and that was when Grace had said to imagine the snake a little baby bunny, happy in the dark, and so she imagines the bunny now, again, and it works, a little, and she writes as many *MP*s as the panes of glass allow, and then she erases them with her same finger and they melt away like nothing, just water, like she was never even here, and then she hears her mother behind her asking if, by chance, the grocery store is still open? There are a few other things she was hoping to buy for dinner, she says, and she knew it had gotten late, but she was hoping if by any lucky chance?

"Maybe," Missy says, not to her mother, and her breath fogs the glass to another clean slate, and she breathes more start-overs, and writes another *MP*.

"*Fantastique!*" Suzanne says.

It is later than the opening. Suzanne waits for Missy to restock the shelves, again, to Scotch tape the prices, again, and reaffix the fruit with the weak Velcro that always takes more time to stick, again. Soon everything will be back in its place—the way Missy liked it, the way Suzanne liked it, and wasn't the snow now so beautiful in the pink light of the sunset? How it blanketed Missy's swing set, and the boxwoods that defined the garden? The little path Suzanne had constructed from stone, gravel, to wander through the allée of pear trees, as if she envisioned Versailles? Missy and Grace had hung the bird feeder on the lowest branch of the sturdiest pear—and Suzanne watches now as a bright red cardinal alights on its perch and sits waiting for something—the train to nowhere? Maybe they're out of the sunflowers that Grace insisted were the best, although Suzanne had always thought Nyjer seeds better, tiny as pepper, for the black and yellow finches. No matter, she thinks, as the cardinal flaps up—perhaps it too has heard the sudden ring of the doorbell, or maybe it just sensed the intensity of Suzanne's gaze, how she willed the scene into a perfect fairytale, or legend: unreal, fantastic, exactly right. Devoid of the gremlins, devoid of everything: glorious and magical.

But when the doorbell rings, it flies away. Someone is here.

"Another customer!" Suzanne says, hurrying to open the door—the cold!—to Grace! Pretty Grace!

"Grace!!" Missy yells, running toward where Grace stands at the entry, snow in her hair, her long, black coat—so New York!—salted with white flakes already melting, her thick mittens caked as if she walked all this way on her hands, her face ruddy, cold, ice on her eyelashes.

"Who wants company?" Grace says.

And they did not have to say that they all did, want company, no one had to say it; they did not have to say that they were all just a little bit lonely. Somehow they knew, and Grace came in and stayed, and the sun went all the way down, and the snow soon melted, and the stars that night, driving home, were brilliant as Grace remembers the cardinal's red now, so many years later, when she on occasion is reminded of Asheville: the smell of the white pine, the feel of Scott's hands on her shoulders, how on the day of the spring snowstorm, she helped Missy write *FERME* on a piece of construction paper to hang above the red cash register that dinged, Missy signing *MP* in the corner of the paper, biting her tongue, and how they had all voted to skip the Bolognese and have cinnamon toast for dinner; and mostly, maybe, how she had finally hiked the trail at the end of the long dirt road before leaving, Mrs. Simpson insisting, to take a look at the famous erratic, following the trees marked with blue ovals, the trail worn but empty, just Grace, alone, past birch in full bloom, their yellow-green leaves and papery white trunks, and wild laurel and rhododendron, until she got to a small clearing and what looked to her like an ordinary stone: just an ordinary stone, an old man or woman of a stone, lichen covered, mossy, tilted on ledge as if against gravity, though she had learned that the stone had been there for millennia, pushed on its path by natural forces—erratics were like that, she had learned, off kilter, precarious: landing wherever they found themselves, balanced against the odds.

Josef Koudelka, Albania. 1994.
Snow blizzard on the road to Korce.
An Albanian braves the weather.

Josef Koudelka, France. Hauts-de-
Seine. Parc de Sceaux. 1987.

GREENEST

JOANNA KLINK

Who is next to me.

Who sees the veil of light laid over the field.

Or the common poppy in the neighbor's yard, such biting
    red a red that blots out other color.

The morning air moored to these chipped steps
    and I can't think or glow into
      anything, left wondering
    if your whole body carries
    tactics—

just some faint hints—
    your murmur of words, too polite,
      the breeze hot that night as we stood
    on the street. I couldn't be sure
    you had smiled.

What is the slightest signal by which
    someone might tell you
    to disappear—

Does the storm threaten the willow's glass leaves

Does sunlight threaten the rain that still falls

The wind can't blow out those roses on the bush—

Wind of firelights! Wind of half-rustled
    sounds. Emissary of a message
      that says you don't even
    need to be here.

———

And I make amends too fast, wanting to
    patch over some rage I feel
      moving toward me
    but can't fully place—the days
    unremarkable—

and I remember we had spoken over dinners,
    talked a little of our work
    and lives—maybe just throwaway lines,
      half-felt, driven by etiquette's
    necessity—

I wake to a motor gunning down the street
    and the drone of a leaf blower
      over warm voices
    of women walking dogs

I wake into the lost parts of a dream, where someone's
    righteous anger finds its footing
      and plots and calculates and makes calls
    barely noticing the swells of rain
      that rolled in today,
    strangely ethereal—
    and writes notes takes meetings

and comes home to find nothing
    but cause—with just a hint of color,
      like my pearl-blue blouse with white
    buttons the glassy light greens
      and dark greens of the young
    soaked garden trees.

———

And it's hard to know how to speak back except to say
    yesterday I was lost

The rainwater wrong, the bones propping up
    my tired body wrong

There is either too much water
    or too much heat

Stricken by what's on the radio a spray of the world's common
    murderous news

and the hanging moss looks like a wet ladder into the oak

My hands propping up my chin, hair knotted, bones
    hollow and light as arrows—
    a great funnel pushed away
      so that I can begin
    another day

The frequencies of morning cold plates and litter
    the numbers on a wall clock the bare
    floor I couldn't be sure
      dim in the electric
    kitchen a sorrow I feel
      anyway despite prospects despite
    better weather—

To what can I turn but the moods of plants and skies
    we both love, or the words
    in books we both love

Canoes like slow jewels on the city's river-water—

and that seagreen luna moth, some iridescent

pink clouds carrying particles of dust
  and gold heat, everything undead
driven by days, low
     rainclouds and the humid
porches screened in against evening
brooding behind a wall

Then the sounds, faint now, of night-knocks and insects

Then the lush silence of midnight where nothing is
                              brisk
    where nothing is hoped for
    or asked

HAMMER OF THE SUN

TIMOTHY DONNELLY

That sound in movies when the lights go on in the football field
    all at once, that thunk that rocks the stadium of night, shudders
alarm across the face of our protagonist, who kneels on turf
    knowing the hand that pulled the switch intends to terrify with this

theatricality of power. It isn't the light per se that scares us here
    but the drastic change in atmosphere, reminding us of how
basic terms of existence can be manipulated so easily, compounded by
    the sudden conspicuousness of one's body on a site designed

for contest and speculation. The message is: we're next, our fate
    sealed on a platform where all outcomes are final. The loud light
watches on in silence now like a god, but one whose cold violet fingers
    sometimes prod a worm of ingenuity to noodle its way through

the interlock of brutal fact—and, after a bit of struggle, set us free.
    Or, more often, not. Circumstances like to be inescapable
and sounds far louder than stadium lights, like the eruption of Krakatoa
    in 1883, so loud it ruptured sailors' eardrums forty miles away,

booming in the western sky in blood-red floods for months, as echoed
    in Munch's masterpiece, whose central figure feels the "infinite
scream passing through nature," as I do the radioactive laughter of the sun
    drunk on splendor, whose hammer I submit to for as long as it takes.

NIGHT OF THE MARIGOLDS

TIMOTHY DONNELLY

Look how the marigolds in the darkness catch the lamplight
    from inside the apartment and bounce it back to us, warning
that we come to be known by the way we respond to
    what we suffer, which is to say by what we have suffered

and not by what we are. In Delacroix's painting of a horse
    frightened by a storm, the animal summarizes thunderclouds
lit by lightning more than horse, unless there's something
    essential to the horse that's unrecognizable as such until

provoked by force. There have been times I've wondered
    about myself, not knowing what it was compared to what
it might have been, or what it isn't, tumbling it over in my mouth
    like raw stone. After a long night of it, if I take the stone

out of my mouth, what surprises me isn't how smooth it is,
    because I expected it to be smooth, but the fact that I have either
troubled it into the shape of a horse, or else sucked away the not-horse
    that kept it from becoming the object it had always meant to be.

Now we are riding into the night. Marigolds towering over us
    drop their scent in waves. Our breathing slows—the horse and I
are in complete communication. The matter of what we mean
    embeds us like a warm Egyptian loam. There's no disputing it.

FICTION

THE DOG STAR
EDWARD MCWHINNEY

———

The world is beautiful. Furthermore, spring is on the way and from where I sit I can see a ship leaving port and I'll call it Dog Star. She flies a flag of the Bahamas and is decked up with multicolored containers. Its gunwales are a rusty red, and the tower is white and blue. She's a lovely vessel. It has a crew of metropolitan marine engineers and merchant seamen; all brave and all cowardly too. Every able seaman is on the run from something. There is no metropolis unknown to him, but he loves the open sea and the thrum of the Mercedes engines that propel the bow through the ocean water. For a moment I am on deck with the fresh sea breeze. I see a school of whales to starboard, flying fish to port, an albatross on the mast. The world is, indeed, beautiful.

My parents died within a week of each other. I sold the house and moved into a room. I found work in a travel agent's. Every day I saw arrangements for planes heading out into the clouds; adventurers bound for travels in exotic lands, families choosing exile or, simply, men off to the races at Cheltenham or Kempton; couples heading for Tenerife.

My own decision to leave Ireland was made easier by so many circumstances; family ties gone; a certain cooling in my girlfriend, Laura, (and her obsession with her studies in hotel management); an assistant bank manager who would tie you into a five-year-fixed before you could say one way to Tangiers.

It was autumn. I sat in the room feeling giddy. I gazed around with a longing. I had bacon and cabbage from Delight's Deli before going out to the streets full of people with laughing faces. I didn't discourage a delusion that it was Paris, London, New York. But it wasn't. It was Cork.

Coming up to Christmas the kerosene ran out and a cold snap rolled in. I sat in my room wrapped in two overcoats. Books remained on the floor, unread, like a line of tasks frozen in a solid row. It was best to get on and read those books and fall into a beautiful absence. Friday after work. All day Saturday. All day Sunday. A long list of forgotten artists flickered on and off like the lights on a Christmas tree.

Laura had left a scarf behind. It smelled strongly of perfume but did nothing to revitalize the memory of her face, which remained an empty shell. I remembered going to the pictures when Captain Marvel was serialized as a short each week. Captain Marvel was in a vast cave, and there was a river of burning lava coming after him. It came not only straight for Captain Marvel but for the screen, threatening all of us sweet suckers with annihilation. Captain Marvel raced for the mouth of the tunnel where the rock gate was descending. The screen went blank. To be continued.

We have been six days at sea. Another six days before the Dog Star is due in port. The drone of the engines is soothing, as is the smell of oil from the next cabin where the telegraphic apparatus is installed, our progress over the depths of the Atlantic recorded by the slow change in wavelength as local news—man armed with hammer and man armed with knife and Lotto player wins half a million and a substantial amount of gold jewelry stolen from a city-center jewelers— gives way to static then calm, slow voices of newsreaders in foreign tongues, reminiscent of childhood turning the dial of longwave radio in the early hours, staccato bursts of world music, crooning jazz, Cuban salsa, then French, Italian, Spanish, maybe Russian, heady mesh of idioms, proportionately thrilling as a meter to fathom the depths below.

I had a bicycle. I cycled into town. When I met people I tried to keep words to a minimum. At least that was the plan. I loved the narrow streets with the postman whistling up and down small gardens. Noisy Yamahas cut the corners. Anything could happen. An exhaust pipe might fall off sending out sparks as from a rocket engine. Chronic drunkards like Marmeladov staggered along. Women wearing slippers, and curlers in their hair; the fag butt in the corner of the mouth, the smoke curling from the jaw over the crown of the head. I tied the bike to a pole and climbed a wall onto the railway line. This would be on a Sunday morning, free from the office, pausing on a hillside to admire the beauty in the distance, beyond the steeples and spires and red smoky rooftops. I felt the breeze with more than a hint of diesel and creosote in it. The silver rails led away into rich, green hills, banks smothered in a blaze of yellow furze come spring.

In Laura, for a time, I was sidelined by the mysterious perfection of an other, meeting on Christmas streets, stars bright, ice blue, her hair still wet, in her new shoes. Sometimes, it felt better staying in the room, linoleum and wood, writing about a walk we took on a beach while she was still interested, watery horizon and kelpy sea air, than going out and becoming entangled in the complications. How much longer? The tide at a low ebb. The motive to continue not always so evident. Her hair with the wet look.

I sat on the windowsill in her bedroom, her parents downstairs. Her garden drenched in rain. So much in the darkness out there. I must jump out the window and fly. Once more the moon was covered over and a drizzle turned to heavy rain, drummed heavy patterns on the roof of the shed. In a few days, in a few hours. I have a confession to make, I said to Laura. I can't sing a note and I can't dance. I should entertain normal dreams like owning a fine car with leather upholstery and ivory fittings and a dashboard like the control center of a nuclear submarine.

In neverending cold I remained undecided, ice-water shave in the dawn, falling out the door. I bought the newspaper along the street, local stories with a universality I chose to minimize. It couldn't happen in Tangiers, Barcelona, or Chicago.

I am afraid of nothing, the merchant seaman writes, on the stormiest day yet. The joists creaks. Anything not screwed down clatters and smashes. It seems I will never become accustomed to these sounds. I am not afraid of creatures from the deep; crazy witches or the legendary Fiji mermaid, comprised of a monkey's torso sewn on to a fish's tail. The ship rocks and creaks, her bowels quiver, sounds like the death rattles of monsters. The lamp flickers.

The room, three stories up, took in light from the street by way of two small windows; droplets of sunshine during the day, neon glowworms by night; a desk, a bookshelf with twenty books. I would have to stay in it for a long time, maybe forever. The city was flooded. I studied a photo of a man floating down Great William O'Brien Street in a wheelie bin. A record volume of water fell from the sky. If it went on so, it could get very scary, the radio broadcaster said. No one needs to see a disaster movie at the present, he continued, we are living in one. People's front rooms were flooded; mattresses, old hats, socks and underpants, who knows what, hairbrushes and false teeth floating around the house.

Laura was suspicious of married men who did not wear marriage bands. Is that so, I said.? If we ever get engaged will you wear a ring? Her father at the table with bread and cheese, the laughing cow, spoke of seagulls attacking people down the docks. He spread the cheese with podgy, little fingers. He spoke of a neighbor whose car alarm had a habit of going off in the early hours.

Later, when she was feeding the cat, I said that I hate cats. I'm allergic to them. My tongue was stilled by a quick glance. It hovered beneath the fragrance of her perfume, the secretion of the civet's anal gland.

When the storm abates, I once more feel in charge of my immediate destiny, that is, I am in charge of the light switch and the radio tuner and I can sit back and listen to the whistling of the second mate through the porthole. I saw him sleeping on a three-legged stool yesterday with his curly head in his hands. He looked like he was holding a cat. The rest of the crew went about their business, a daily clamor drawn from an eternal pattern. It's always the same, never the same, like each swell of the sea, always, never. The men drink coffee laced with brandy and rum, and from this remove their murmur is the same as it was yesterday, nothing about it to distinguish one day from the next.

The chef breathes tobacco smoke through the porthole of the galley, dreaming of a girl with buttons on her dress. He learns French and Spanish and Portuguese from phrasebooks, one expression per day, calculating how many charming sentences he will know by the time we reach Valparaiso.

We drove out to Weaver's Point in Laura's Micra. She was quiet, looking for swans and egrets in the estuary along the way, hoping to spot a whale or a school of dolphins when we got to the point. She wore a new hat and a natty tweed jacket. She was as composed as the manager of a four-star hotel. On the way home she became more talkative. What would you like for your birthday, she asked? A birthday cake, I replied. Well, that's easy, but I mean what present would you like? How about a typewriter that talks, I said? I guessed that she already had something bought, probably a shirt and tie, held together in a plastic box with a score of tiny pins.

When the flood waters abated, I went for a walk along the railway line. The city covered in smog seemed to be floating on more than water. The spires of St. Finbar's, Holy Trinity, Shandon, and the North Cathedral stuck up out of it. Something was changing in my head. There was a vague idea of slipping silently and unnoticed away from the conventions, becoming a vagrant, wandering around the globe somehow in anonymity. I observed two types and thought about them in the ignorant language of a twenty-year-old, those who dreamed of fame and wealth and power and those soft-spoken men with leery eyes, beery breaths, and wives with pregnant bellies. I stepped into a bar and fell into shadows as powerful as echoes along hollow walls, up to the ceiling where they twist with the smoke and paint, where the paint warps until nothing is heard but noise.

Laura's mother made skirts and kidney stew. After eating I went to talk with her sixteen-year-old brother, Noah, who was writing a science-fiction novel about the Planet Pett, which has a twenty-four-year day followed by a twenty-four-year night. I overheard snippets of an argument in the kitchen, Laura and her mother; sighs, angry suppressed voices. I left. As I walked I felt my head spin. I made my way to the Ferry House, clouds of smoke, kegs of alcohol, where sailors gathered and whores and where the confusion in my head was calmed. The spring was on its way.

The gray smog came in the open window. It, too, will evaporate; nothing is permanent. I slept on the linoleum floor with books for bedclothes. The smog turned blue. It would be wiser to take life by its scruffy neck and change it before it changes itself.

It was late April. On the table, my passport and airline ticket. Laura's final word in my ears. We had parted in Delight's Deli. We should never have met, she said. You're so young. God bless. She was young too but she spoke those words like an old aunt. God Bless. I'll think of you.

We will reach port tomorrow. We celebrate our last night at sea with bottles of Guinness and beef stroganoff, with South African wine and German schnapps.

FICTION / KAYLA BLATCHLEY

A BODY IN MOTION

AND THEN SHE TURNED.

She sees a mother shoving her boy, her flat hand against the back of his head, the two of them walking down the sidewalk, the boy in front of her, at a quick pace. She is yelling. He has done wrong; he has ruined it. He has let the cat out of the house again. He was careless and didn't look behind him as he was stepping out and now the cat is houses down, hiding under the belly of a car or tucked in some bush. Two other kids stand in front of the house, backpacks loose on their shoulders, still as sticks.

The mother is fast. She is too quick she barks, her legs and arms triangles of movement. Now they'll be late for school. They will miss their bus. Get my keys, get my keys out of my purse, now.

They had been walking toward the cat that had run away, the boy and the mom were. The mom was ahead, and then she turned.

Now look what you've done. You never listen, and she pointed back to the house. He starts walking back to it and she walks up behind him, faster, always faster, taller, bigger. And he's walking away and she's yelling and she reaches out, palm spread, and shoves his head.

His body goes forward and down. He has to skip and catch himself from falling.

FORWARD AND DOWN.

Her face found pavement outside of the concert on the pathway leading out. She had tried to put her shoulder to it when she saw she was falling, and did not let go of her cigarette, but she landed cheekbone scratched into the dusty cement and bleeding; a swollen eye the next day. She got up and they had laughed. She had been careless and couldn't see in front of her; there was such confusion of light and dancing and getting at something she didn't have but wanted.

She finished smoking her cigarette as her friend's son wiped the blood from her cheek, and they laughed together. She wanted the moment to last forever.

Her cheek burning, her doing a good job of standing up and brushing it off. She'd been careless; letting herself get this way.

THE MOTHER IS FAST.
She is too quick, she barks. Now they'll be late for church. She remembers the swerving of the car, that motion taking a turn too quick and their bodies in the car falling, trying to adjust. The mother swerves into a lane in oncoming traffic in bright light. They hadn't listened, and now they are late again. The harsh words barking out; what they haven't done, how they've disappointed her.

She's yanked the leash on her dog. Keeping him safe from harm but recognizing the anger in it. She has yanked so hard his head twists.

There is broken glass on the sidewalk, the stove is hot, they could run out into the street if they don't listen and what happens then?

The eldest knows better, and should have looked out for the cat, should've helped getting his younger brother and sister ready as he knows he needs to do, as he has done every morning. Is it too much to ask of him? What choice does she have. She points back to the house.

He was careless and didn't look behind him as he was stepping out and now the cat is houses down, hiding under the belly of a car or tucked in some bush. Two other kids stand in front of the house, backpacks loose on their shoulders.

Now they'll be late for school. They will miss their bus.

———

Something she didn't have but wanted. What was it? They had been walking toward.

Now look what you've done. You never listen, and she pointed back to the house.

Faster, always faster, taller, bigger. Two other kids stand in front of the house, backpacks loose on their shoulders, still as sticks. He has let the cat out of the house again. He has to skip and catch himself from falling. She wanted that moment to last forever.

THIS FALL

LYNN MELNICK

I wear a moth-eaten sweater dress
and refuse to speak in metaphor.
One of these days I will sew up the holes.
One of these days

I will learn how to sew
so I can sew up the holes.
I do things with my body
I am ashamed to tell you about

but not ashamed to have done.
I go into and out of
the city on the subway.
I am already in the city but

I go into the center.
People like to ask me for directions
so we can get lost together.
I await word

from a love in the hospital
but word doesn't come.
I am trolled on Twitter
for complaining about men.

Is it too early in the century to write
trolled on Twitter into a poem
because I'm pretty sure *trolled on Twitter*
will be in my obituary

and in that of our century.
I'm wearing it well, moth-eaten.

They think I think
I'm too good for men, which

I have always been. Still,
I find myself opening my heart.
I would like to be rescued
from these feelings

while I resist revealing
what it feels like in a body
awaiting word and waiting
for my husband

to get home from the city.
My challenge is to stop bracing
for the worst. We are lost.
Every love like all of us will die.

I will never get word.
I will wait and wait
for my husband to arrive
with the vindictive wind

into the fourth floor of what is also
the city. I'm bleeding
more than I ever have,
each bleed worse than the last,

my immoderate body
at the crest of things. I'm bleeding
in abundance onto my dress
and onto the couch.
When I was in school I wrote
a poem called "Blood Stains."
My teacher wrote *not quite*

across the top

but blood does stain, quite.
On Twitter a man calls me ugly.
On Twitter another man
calls me a bitch.

I've never been either
but I could stand to be both.
I wait obsessively for word.
I am invincible and

I am so sorry, Twitter.
I hear news—
I hear news!—
from the hospital: *I'm ok*.

I feel my body relax
inside the waning
worst-case-scenario reel.
This is the century *overwhelm*

became a noun, isn't it?
If my heart has to be open let it
at least sometimes receive relief.
I peel off my dress at the kitchen sink.

My husband walks in
and my body unspools further.
If I ask him, he will know how
to stitch the hole in my dress.

I told you I'm not speaking in metaphor.
I warned you we are all going to die.

A JEWISH CHRISTMAS IN PALM SPRINGS

LYNN MELNICK

If you ask me why all my poems
are the same I'll admit all my
impulses are sexual and all my
grudges are biblical. Skip my bio,
I'll just tell you: I took a woman
to the desert and she slapped
my red mouth in a dander. I took
a man to the desert and he died
in front of me puffed up under
an obscene feast of stars muffled
by holiday strings of outsize bulbs
among the cacti. Sure, I'm duly
bowled by such grandeur but
I am asking you for patience
while I learn to say what I saw.

GREAT QUESTION

LISA OLSTEIN

When I say seeing you again really opened me up
I mean like a hatchet to the chest

I keep hidden in my chest, stuck drawers
near the heart. Little lathe, long past,

do you remember? After years of careful study
and even more studied looking away,

having retraced the memory palace
from the unfinished novel of what lives

and lives and lives and still lives
wherever it is flint meets spark in the dark,

hot orange here then gone low and slow,
a smoldering field, a controlled burn—

yes, I remember. Finally,
I've located the girl, the bend, the night,

that series of precise and fumbling distances
that set our bodies in motion

across thousands of other nights but
from these forensics I've gleaned no wisdom

only wish, sorrow, sorrow, wish,
nothing at all about the ox I am or my cart.

THE DISASTER AGAIN

LISA OLSTEIN

The intensity of it, that distantness
that keeps watch. Bereft of light,

absence refers endlessly to the other
law, the disaster again in motionless

flight: the four winds from nowhere,
the night, the lure of it, the night,

the thought of it, disastrous already.
Dreaming, something wakes, a sliding

half-gleam in a devastated field,
disastrous return. Then we who are

turned away from the star wake gently.
That there is nothing disastrous in this

is surely what we must learn to think.
This, too, is fatal or, as they say, inevitable—

the absence linked to the disaster, fragmentary,
posterior to every possibility yet to come.

THAT'S THE PAIN YOU HAVE

A pitiful little snow fell in the night. The morning was bleak, cold, and the sky was still milk-gray just before noon.

"Heard there was ice on the bridge," Griswold said, by way of greeting.

"Not just there," Pytor had been listening to the radio on his way from the art building. A truck went off one of the turns on the way from Cedar Rapids and plunged into an embankment near the river. He'd been carrying a bunch of chickens, some of which drowned in the icy water.

They were on the first floor of the gym, which smelled like old leather and sweat. They climbed to the third-floor racquetball courts, and shucked themselves of their sweats, but left on their quarter zips while they warmed up. The ball had left faint crescents of dust and blue paint on the white back wall like bruises. Griswold had a mean, stinging forehand that cracked the silence in the cell, like a gunshot, like mortar fire. *Bang, bang, bang*. Pytor stretched while he watched Griswold take his practice cuts. Pytor had learned to play racquetball relatively recently. He had spent most of his life playing lacrosse, and so certain of the motions came easily to him. He had the eyes and the hands for the game, but sometimes his strides were too big, and he tumbled over or slammed into the wall. He felt clumsy in the enclosed room in a way he never did on the field. Griswold was faster than he looked, thick as he was with muscle. And he leapt and dove and struck with brutality from positions where it seemed unlikely. But both of them played with the raw, still unfinished strokes of hobbyists, and they were more in danger of harming themselves than displaying real mastery over the game.

Pytor stood and caught the ball on his racquet right before it reached Griswold, who had reared back to take another swing.

"Don't be greedy," he said, and Griswold laughed. Pytor dropped in for his own warm up, Griswold sat to stretch behind him. The ball was coming quickly today. It smelled new, with the white powder from the bottle. It was a lively ball, and Pytor relaxed his grip and changed the angle so that more of the ball's power was absorbed at impact. It slowed marginally, and he could control it then, sending it from side to side, warming first his forehand and then his backhand. He stepped in and ripped a one-handed drive directly up the line of the wall into the corner where it struck and died, went dead still. Griswold whistled behind him.

"Someone's a killer today."

Pytor liked that, swelled with pride at the compliment, which was rare from Griswold. Not that Griswold was particularly rude or mean, but he was selfish when he played. When Pytor brought this up to him once, Griswold's face sank and he said that it was because he'd learned to play when he was in college, and he'd gotten his ass kicked by the doctors who worked at the medical complex across the street. They played the blunt, aggressive game of men accustomed to masturbating quietly and rigidly into socks on the edge of their beds. When they struck the rubber ball, it flew so hard and so close to the floor that it was sometimes indistinguishable from the lines that marked the court. When he played, he was always playing the ghosts of those men, cutting them down before they saw where he was exposed and ended him. In this way, Pytor pitied and understood Griswold, and the few compliments that Griswold paid him meant something because he knew they had been dispensed with great difficulty.

The two of them had been playing racquetball together for about six months. Griswold had recently moved back to town after a brief and unsuccessful tenure in biotech at a company called Ceto. The company specialized in a variety of diagnostic tests—for pregnancy, for migraine, for the onset of a common cold, for UTI, for diabetes, for measles. All it took was a single drop of blood and a little bit of spit, and the secrets of your body scissored open to be inspected like the genitalia of some minor sea creature. It seemed remarkable to Griswold that one company could test for such a range of ailments, and he suspected there was some fuzz around the edges. That is, he thought they were a sham, the way all companies are. The whole of biotech was a series of brightly illuminated store fronts at the back of which were dank and dismal people carrying out routine tasks at a markup that was less than ethically sound. But he also thought that there must be something to it, after all. Not so much because Ceto had raised a great deal of venture capital (it was not difficult to convince people who knew nothing about biology that anything was possible), but perhaps because when he took the samples each day and loaded them into the patented machine, he felt a little flicker of hope as it whirred to life and ran a series of data across his screen. Certainly, *something* was happening.

The process was simple. A person could go to any Ceto kiosk and receive a testing kit. The idea was that if you were feeling a little funny or wanted to know if you were on the cusp of something awful, all you had to do was stumble into one of the slender, gray kiosks like a phone booth, but ovular. You didn't even have to type your name. All you had to do was slot connect your cellular device and grant it permission to access your contacts. Then, you pricked your finger and spat in a tube, and slotted these into the machine where they were barcoded and cooled. Late at night, Ceto technicians scurried around town collecting the samples and bringing them to a local hub, where the samples were shipped overnight, on dry ice, to the main office. And it was there, at his airtable, that Griswold carefully and delicately tested the samples. It was moronic work, he said. Pipetting and clicking *Yes, Go!* on the interface. Anyone could have done it with minor training. Griswold had foolishly said at lunch once, *Imagine, you could get homeless people in here and train them how to use a pipette, and like, really do something.* But then, someone had said, *But they're homeless* as if that explained it. When your sample was tested and your profile generated, you could access it from anywhere by logging into your account. Client data was stored on their servers indefinitely. Even if you deleted your account, the data remained, like a severed limb.

It had been a bright and useless period in his life. He went to work. He went home to an apartment in a building from the fifties. He cooked small dinners for himself, which he ate by the window, watching the traffic and sometimes, at just the right moment in just the right way, he could see Lake Michigan. Or, the bare outline of Lake Michigan. His time in Chicago was brief, however. It turned out that he had been correct, and that Ceto was a scam. Not the science, which as it happened, was actually quite sound. Instead, the chief executives of the company had been engaging in a low level of securities fraud, and Ceto collapsed down like the cardboard boxes out of which Griswold had extracted his desk chair.

Griswold wanted to serve first, and Pytor had no objections. The serve was Griswold's worst stroke, not because it lacked power but because Griswold lacked full control over it. The serve often hit high on the wall or it floated. Sometimes, it was more a kill shot than a serve—Griswold not the tactical kind exactly—but mostly, Pytor could handle it. Griswold didn't have the wisdom to know this about himself, that his serve put him in a weak position, or maybe he did know and just wanted to get it out of the way. There was no way of really knowing exactly. They began and sure enough Griswold leaned into one up the sidewall line and it struck low and tight to the floor, close enough that if it had been late in the game, Pytor would have asked for a redo but as it was, it was early, and so he let it go. He settled into a crouch and waited for the next one, and when it came, higher up the wall, with a rebound in the short court, plenty of pace to carry it back to him, he struck evenly and decisively, killing the ball to the opposite corner and putting Griswold off balance. So they began, taking points from each other, in that jerky, stiff early phase of the game, when the loud echoes had no rhythm and their feet were still cold.

Pytor served with placement, focusing more on clean, direct strokes, trying to make Griswold run because he lacked stamina overall and his balance was suspect, and it was usually around the middle of the first set that Pytor's strategy paid off and he wedged control of the game steadily, at first imperceptibly, into his own hands. Griswold was occasionally brilliant in his aggression and occasionally silly, and at one point he ended up with his legs stretched high above his head against the plastic wall because he'd gone rolling and tumbling to catch the ball before it landed, and sure enough, he'd whipped the ball with such vicious force and spin that it had sank and kissed the backwall, and spun violently away from Pytor who had been too distracted by Griswold's body position to notice what was happening until it was too late. But it was a futile thing because Pytor won that set handily, and they started the second.

The problem with playing Griswold was that he was a genius of second sets. His focus tightened and he deployed strategies that he had seemed incapable of before, and because he was so strong he could wrench shots from ridiculous situations and no matter how coolly and thoughtfully Pytor sent him skidding and running, there was nothing to derail because he had too much power and too much determination. And on that day in particular, he played like something crucial was at stake, and Pytor lost the second set in a blow-out, narrowly avoiding the mercy rule.

They took a break then and sat with their backs against the clear wall. Pytor's shirt stuck to his back in a wet way that made him queasy to contemplate. Griswold took his shirt off and wrung it out. The air in the cell had grown humid from their bodies and their game. Griswold mopped up his sweat so that they wouldn't slip on it. Pytor wasn't winded. But his thighs burned and his elbows ached, and his wrist had a dull, good pain. He had tripped on the last shot of the set and caught himself by slapping the side wall, which had caused an old callus to split open. But it didn't hurt. It just opened and closed like the skin of a fruit and when he poked at it, he marveled at how thick it was. Pytor was a sculptor, a potter more than anything else. But he had, in an earlier phase of his life, been what he called a real sculptor. By which he meant that he had worked in stone and other hard materials. He had been attracted to it as a child because it seemed like the sort of thing that was impossible to do casually, and he craved serious things because he wanted people to respect him. No one respected the young or considered them particularly knowing about what they wanted or needed from life, and so he had grafted himself onto stonework because it was time and resource intensive, and sure enough, his parents and his teachers had quietly approved from the periphery as he apprenticed to a master stoneworker and sculptor over the summers in Minnesota. But then, when he was seventeen, the master stoneworker was sent to prison for possession of several pieces of child pornography, including pictures of Pytor, which Pytor had sent him thinking they were innocent reference photos for a piece the stoneworker claimed to have been working on. And so in the cold, clammy bathroom of his parents' house just outside of Minneapolis, he had stripped down from his lacrosse gear and taken pictures of his skinny chest and arms, and legs, and he'd sent them over email. It didn't feel like betrayal for the reasons people thought it did—it felt like betrayal to Pytor because he had thought the master stoneworker actually valued him enough to want to make art from his body and valued him as a pupil and a student. It felt like a betrayal because something that had seemed to be about art and the fullfiment of Pytor's wish to be taken seriously by adults had been turned into something ugly and small and evil. He felt bad that he would never see those little pieces he'd sculpted ever again, as if they were the toll for admission into some dark, unpleasant knowledge about adulthood.

Now Pytor worked in clay. The irony of it did not escape him. Griswold leaned forward to stretch out his back. Pytor leaned over and pushed down at him. Griswold groaned and gave in.

"Hurts," he said.

"Don't be a baby."

Griswold grunted at him and Pytor tossed him a towel.

"You're wet," he said. Pytor breathed and shook out the numbness his legs. He bounced the ball hard, fast, and he tried to make his vision settle. Griswold lumbered up and cracked his shoulders and neck. He was playing the final set without a shirt on, Pytor thought. A mean-spirited impulse rose in him, quickly, a desire to send the ball hard directly into his back, to see if it left a bruise or if Griswold yelped in pain. But the desire was gone almost before it had cohered fully. What was left was something akin to desire, fuzzy and indistinct, like an idea for a pot or a mug, like an idea for something that he might make if only he had the resolve. Griswold looked at him then, and there was, between them, a moment of great tension. It felt like they were pulling on the ends of something, and the air grew taut, under the harsh lights, and the world came back to them. Pytor could hear the game next door, the thunderous footsteps, the bangs of the balls striking the wall, the shouts of exertion. They were not alone. The tension eased, and Pytor turned to serve.

The final set went easy enough for Pytor. He mechanically unmade Griswold's defenses, and watched as he crashed into the walls like being jerked around on the end of a string. It didn't bother him after a while, but then Griswold fought back, and they were level, at match point. Their breathing was heavy, their bodies sore, and Pytor served one hard time, a kill shot, a perfect ace.

At the art building, Pytor sat in the break room. The air had grown colder outside on his way back from the gym with Griswold. The radio in the small office played the news, and Griswold changed out of his sweats into jeans. He changed his socks and left them on the radiator to dry. He toweled his face and his hair as best he could. He felt clean and bright. Astringent. The heat of the game still burned under his skin like a private heat source, and he pulled on his apron, tying it himself in the way he hated to tie it because it felt clumsily made and like it would come undone at any moment, which bothered him, distracted him.

He sat at his little desk in the corner and sketched for a few minutes, diffuse, nonsense sketches. He was in the middle of a longish project that involved the creation of a series of jugs. Cartoonishly long, too long to be of real utility. He wanted to take a common form, an ancient form, the repository meant for eventual distribution, and to stretch it to see to what lengths he could go before it became only a caricature of itself. The project had come because he'd realized that much of computer iconography—the save icon, folder icon, the fact of documents being called files, in the first place—came from physical artifacts that had been reproduced digitally not because they were actually useful forms in that way but because they represented something, signified something and so the once functional utility of the form had been subsumed into the referential, and the referential into the playful, into a meme. And so a jug was a jug until it was a decoration. It reminded one of a jug, the form being an icon, being a thing whose shape suggested utility, until one tried to enact utility with it. What he wanted was to reproduce the digital meme-ification of things but in the physical, in the lasting, a comment upon ephemera etched in permanent materials. But not too permanent. Clay. Sustainable, with eco-consciousness glazes. The very process of firing, however, dangerous, yes, toxic, bad, but that could be circumvented carefully, thoughtfully, conscientiously. He was not an idiot. Not a buffoon. He knew things.

Pytor's notebooks were full of sketches of jugs, some top-heavy, some bottom-heavy, some with shafts as long as his arms. He sometimes left the joining exposed, a comment on process, which was a thing that people liked to see because it gave them something to *talk about*, made them feel that their mind was capable of agile processing. His favorite part of the process was when the jugs were leather hard and capable of supporting their own weight. Then he carved away at them, shaving away layers, planing until they were smooth and thin and quite fragile. He liked to cut out shapes from their necks, which made pouring impossible, and it was this tension that most intrigued him. The impulse to pour, the physical impossibility of it. Then there were the jugs that were actually capable of pouring. These he made sensible and compact and he sent home to his mother and to his aunts and his grandmothers. They kept them in their kitchens and used them for tea and lemonade and water. They used them in the summer and the winter. And when he went home for the holidays, they kissed his cheeks and poured from his jugs and handed him the mugs he had made for them.

The grad office belonged to him and the other pottery and ceramics RAs. It adjoined the small studio where they made their smaller works and stored the spare clay and where sometimes Martine taught illegal pottery lessons at night. By some strange unspoken understanding, the other RAs had agreed not to sell her down the river to the faculty, in no small part because they each had their own side hustles. For spare money, Pytor donated sperm to in-need couples. He'd deposit his sample into a little sterile cup and would ship it overnight on dry ice across the country. The first time he had done it, he had been surprised at the ease of it. There was a kit online. People paid him well. Sometimes, he thought about all of the children out there he had made. Or not made. This shadowy legion of people who were related to him. Who might be awkward and left-handed like him. Too serious too young. Easy bleeders when stuck at the doctor's office. But mostly he did not think about them.

He sketched Griswold's broad back as he had seen it at the start of the last set. He sketched in the shadows of bruises. The long channel of his spine, the two columns of muscle and flesh that rose on either side of it. His shoulders. The curly, dark hair, the tilt of his head so that his chin sank just a little under the shoulder and the eyes peeking back, catching the observer. It was a quick but focused sketch and it contained some of the moment that had passed between them in the cell, some of the tension he had felt when Griswold looked at him. Some of the sensation that had come over him, that had made him want to do harm just to see what would happen. It was a familiar sensation, one that came over him when he passed the rows and rows of curing pottery. Sometimes, he wanted to tilt the racks over and send it all tumbling down to the floor, to hear the crash and break of it, as if that might cause time to come out of joint and flatten before him. He had wanted to harm Griswold. Not for any reason, nothing particularly interesting or worthy. But simply to see what might happen.

When he was done, he put on his moccasins. He went into the small studio and sat in what dim light washed in through the windows. It was quiet. The whole building had settled into a deep stillness all around him. Ice against the window. A distant siren winging its way out toward the edge of town.

He did not throw. He did not make anything. He sat there until it was dark. Until the ambient light from down the hall thrown against the door like a pale shadow was his only way of seeing. Everyone else was on winter break. He, alone, sat in the building. And if he was not alone, he had no way of knowing that he was not.

It was him and only him, sitting in the dark. In the whole world. He felt a little better to consider it.

At the café downtown, he met Griswold, who was still sweating. He said he had run there from his apartment over the river. Pytor laughed at him, but he knew that Griswold had done it to help himself kick a bad habit.

For a long time, Griswold had been trying to get well. He gave up smoking and drinking. He gave up red meat. Then he gave up refined sugar and salt. He drank only water, which he sometimes supplemented with pale electrolyte powder. On his bedside table, he kept a notebook where he jotted down his calories and the liters of fluid he drank each day. In the way that his grandfather, a preacher, had taught him to pray each morning and night, Griswold reached for the book and read the numbers off quietly to himself, adding finally the day's tally at the end. Then he would close the book and turn out the light, and descend into the promise of unbroken sleep. This was the shape of his life. It did not bring him misery or hope. If he got better, he did not know. It was as if his life were a specimen trapped between two slips of glass. This was what he had, he said. A list of things given up. A list of things consumed. A dip into darkness at the end of each day. If the world held no mystery for Griswold, it was because he had lost the capacity for looking at it, having come out of the world.

Each morning, Griswold jogged approximately three miles. The houses stooped under the veil of darkness like small, fearful mammals. Occasionally, there was a light on in a bedroom or a kitchen, and it was like seeing a star blaze into life, so total was the darkness. He ran along his residential street toward the park, which was a circular clump of a grass on a hill with a gazebo that looked winded, like it was trying to catch its breath. Running up the hill, Griswold felt the fibers of his muscles stretch, the angle of gravity shift. There is a moment when one is shifting uphill, where the body is confused, and the angle of impact on the pavement is correct but not correct, before the body adjusts, and for perhaps only a step or two, there is a sensation like falling or existing outside of gravity, like going for a step that doesn't exist, a bead of thrilling fear. Griswold lived for that moment.

In the park, he did a few laps around the track, swinging his arms through the cold and watching the birds glide back and forth across the tips of the trees. When he returned home, the world was gray, slashed through with light, and he saw other people's lives through snatches in their windows, each like a blurred portrait. He thought that sometimes of taking pictures while in motion. Pictures of people in their windows as he ran by. He thought of compiling these blurry snapshots and asking what of them was human. What could one extrapolate from these hazy outlines, the suggestion of people-forms. It amused him, like one of those jokes with no real punch line, the kind of joke that tapers off at the end into shy laughter—*two old men walk into a hardware store, and you know*. A series of portraits that were not portraits.

Pytor could understand that. The slant rhyme of it. Thing and not thing, somehow contained within each other. Like a metaphor. Pytor had espresso. Griswold had a seltzer. They sat near the fireplace. Which Pytor thought might be too warm for Griswold, but Griswold just waved that concern off.

"Anyway," he said. "I have a question for you."

"I perhaps have an answer, but no promises," Pytor said.

The café was empty, which was not surprising because the undergraduates has cleared out. They went home. To places like Des Moines and Ames and Cedar Rapids and Waterloo and Davenport and to Illinois. They left and returned to their families. But Pytor had not returned home. Some people stayed. People like him and Griswold who had been left stranded by a sudden and violent receding of life's currents.

"I fell off a stool out at my aunt's place," Griswold started to say. "It hurt pretty fucking bad. I went to the doctor, and the doctor says, it's a little broken."

"I didn't know a leg could be a little broken."

"Me either," Griswold say, puffing out his cheeks. "Anyway, he says it will be okay, just stay off it, you know."

"And this was when exactly?"

"Back in the summer. It was bad. It was so hot in that house," Griswold said, shaking his head and blotting his brow. He startled briefly, realizing that his forehead was damp with sweat, as if the sudden collision of memory and the present, their instantaneous blurring together, had somehow caught him by surprise. "Anyway, I go, he gives me these pills."

Pytor nodded. He did not know what this story had to do with anything that Griswold might ask of him. He felt a diffuse and shifting nervousness, like arriving at a test unprepared.

"Anyway, I didn't take them. Leg's fine. It's okay. I just tough through it, you know?"

"Right," Pytor said.

Griswold then removed from his coat pocket a small bottle of pills that rattled when he shook them. He set them on the table between them like putting out a business card.

"So I have them. Still."

"Right," Pytor said.

"And, like, I'm not going to take them."

"Yeah."

"Is it… unethical to like. Sell them? Just to people who *really, really* need them?"

Pytor whistled, loudly, too loudly for the empty café and the baristas looked at them. Pytor briefly saw how they must have looked then, with the pill bottle on the table between them. And there was a desire in him to want to cover them up, to hide them from view, but that would have been *more* suspicious, not *less*, and so he did nothing.

"Ethically? I don't know. But I'm pretty sure it's illegal."

"Yeah, I'm not really… I mean, the law, whatever. I'm talking about people's pain."

"Okay, yeah, "I hear that."

"Do you?"

"Yeah," Pytor said. "I just meant, I didn't think about *ethical*, I mean. That seems secondary to getting caught selling controlled substances."

"Nevermind," Griswold said. "Never fucking mind. God, why did I even ask?"

Pytor's face grew red. He did not understand the flaring up of emotion in this particular context, why it was that Griswold was inflamed with feeling. It had seemed an innocuous question, something simple even if the answer itself was complicated and not easily sorted into a right or wrong answer. But still, he leaned back in his chair and put his hands up in a posture of passive vulnerability.

"I'm on your side," Pytor said. "I'm not judging you."

Griswold's shoulders relaxed, but his face remained closed. He sat up a little straighter.

"I'm sorry,"he said. "I know that. But it feels like people are always judging me. It's how it feels. It's persistent. It's painful. No matter what I do or how hard I try, I'm still, like, judged. Because I was on pills. Because I washed out of my life. Whatever. People make up their minds about you and that's it. That's the pain you have. Forever."

"I know what that's like," Pytor said, thinking of the master sculptor, of the way he had been molded into his life, made into one thing and not allowed to change. Thinking of the ways his family watched him, carefully, with great attention and fear, looking out for all the cracks and breaks and chips and jagged edges, all of the ways that he might suddenly reveal what hidden details lay inside of him. He thought of how when people found out about the master sculptor, what they did was one of two things, either pity him or blame him, sometimes both, very rarely neither. And how he feared it getting out and people knowing it because it curtailed all of the other things they might come to know and love and understand about him. Pytor knew what it was to have a single painful fact become the whole of your person so that even you doubted yourself, your character, your feelings. He knew.

"Somehow I doubt that," Griswold said, but he pressed, saying also, "But these pills. I mean. I should not have taken them. I shouldn't have been given them. But I was. And I've managed not to re-up, you know. I have. I have been *good*. I have been so fucking good. But I think, sometimes, I have to get rid of them. So why not help people in pain. And help myself too."

"You could donate them," Pytor said. "Shelters, right?"

Griswold nodded slowly, like this fact had occurred to him and been dismissed before. "Just seems like, I don't know. I could use the money."

"Then sell them," Pytor said.

"But what if I sell them to the wrong person. What if someone like me comes up and gets them, and it's just, back into their veins. I mean, fuck."

"I think that you never know what someone else is feeling or going through," Pytor said. "People are responsible for themselves. They know what they can and can't handle."

"That's not always true," Griswold said, and Pytor flushed with shame at that because he knew how true that was.

"But you can't know when they don't know," Pytor said. "I try to always err on the side of letting people tell me when they need help."

Griswold sighed and folded his arms like a surly child, and Pytor again thought of the moment during racquetball when he had wanted to hit him hard, as hard as he could, with the ball. He thought of the moment in the café with the empty gray quiet swirling around them, and it was like they were in the cell again, just the two of them, on the slick, gleaming floors, the firm rubber in his hands, the racquet, the impulse to maim, to strike, to do harm, to cause pain. He thought of then, as surely as he had felt that morning, and the two moments in his life were connected by a single, vibrating string of recollection, joined as if physically connected, one pulling steadily on the other, and he couldn't escape the sensation, the overpowering feeling that one was evolving into the other, like then, right then, he might do something horrible to Griswold. He wondered, bleakly, if this was the same channel through which all genuine human connection flowed. If pain and charity and love and understanding all moved through the same, thin bridges connecting moments to moments and lives to other lives.

"Should I or should I not?"

"I think you should do whatever you want, Griswold. And if it feels bad, I don't know, maybe don't."

"That's very Sunday school," Griswold said.

"I guess it is."

"Alright." Griswold took the pills off the table and put them back into his pocket. They finished their coffee and went out into the gray, scraping cold. They were going in opposite directions. Griswold hugged him tightly. He had a metallic smell, like copper. Pytor patted his back and then his shoulders, and he tried to extricate himself, but he could not. They stood on the sidewalk holding each other a while. Cars passed. Across the street, a great, hulking machine was digging out a gravel pit, and its crew of resigned men in yellow coveralls watched them with flinty eyes. Griswold let him go.

"See you," Pytor said.

"See you," Griswold said, his voice a little quiet, a little sad, and then he was gone, moving down the street toward the grocery store, and then beyond under the veil of trees that adjoined the hospital parking lot.

The men in the construction site across the street were still watching him, as though they expected something, and Pytor, not knowing what to do or say to them, squared his shoulders and went on. He thought of that curious moment many times over the next week and month and year. He thought of it again and again, when it had seemed that he had been asked something important and had blanked. A moment when he had failed to rise to meet something put to him. By both the men in the site across the street and by Griswold, who he never heard from again.

It wasn't until he was living in Madison, years and years later, that he heard from a mutual friend, the very friend who had taken Griswold to the hospital after the fall in his aunt's house, that Griswold had been found a couple weeks later dead, from an overdose. It was an ugly fact, ugly because of its simplicity and its directness. The friend had been passing through Wisconsin on the way from Michigan down into Iowa. Pytor had put her up on his fold-out in the living room. He was living with a man then. But the friend and Pytor, sitting across from one another late one night, drinking whiskey which he never did, talking about people they knew, had landed on Griswold. Grizzy, she said, her face falling. God. And then all of it had come out. And Pytor thought if only he had said something different. If only he had given him something else, something more. If only. He'd felt so bad about it. And also confused because that part of his life, when he lived in Iowa and knew Griswold, when he had gone out of graduate school and into the world, no longer fit into the life he had now, in Madison, making plates for a local hotel chain and restaurant. None of it fit together. This was the geometry of his life. Not a line. Nor a set of spheres nested inside of each other. But a jagged and weird assemblage of fragments.

He and the friend fucked on the creaking fold-out in muted, hostile sadness. And then she was gone, and that part of his life lifted out and left him, and it was as though the awful knowledge of knowing what had happened to Griswold had been stored away. Like all of the jugs from his thesis show, sitting in the dim compartment of his mother's garage in Minneapolis.

The nature of pain, Pytor thought as the friend pulled away in her small, blue Honda, was that, essentially. It waited in the dark, waiting, perhaps, to be of some use.

SUNSHOWER

It's the last poem in the unit.

The school year wears thin, an inchoate Christmas smell in the air: salty Australian sunlight and eucalyptus and dry heat. The poem has too many big words. *Cumulus, petrified, syncopated,* a halting journey over multisyllabic hills.

My old private school students would be whining, giving up. But class 12B pushes on, relentless, through *gouts* and *ped-e-stals* and *rei… rei… reiterative.*

Most transferred from the Intensive English Center nearby. Until I packed my life up and took the train line out west, I'd never met teenagers so gentle, or with such old eyes, whose faces lit up just from learning a new word.

"*Rack on rack,*" I read, as we inch across each stanza, pages filling with the beautiful, looping script of students used to writing in Arabic and Tamil. "Anish?"

"Repetition!"

"Yes! And this line, Nazem?"

"Simile, Miss."

"Fantastic! And *bacon redness of bark…*?"

Here, things go sideways.

Of every image used in the poet's description of a bushwalk, I thought this one would be easy to grasp. Maybe it's the stagnant heat, or the arduous journey through unfamiliar vocabulary. Metaphor, they decide, but what's it *mean*? The entire poem collapses—the sandstone *puffed like fungi,* the *broken iceberg* cliff, trunks of *caterpillar green.*

"Why he calls it that?"

"Miss, why he is on the walk?"

Bacon. Redness. Bark. They know the words. But why here, why together?

We Google a Sydney red gum; they don't agree it resembles bacon, declare it "ugly" and "looking like a sunburn."

The bell rings. On Monday we pick up where we left off. I've brought a strip of curling rind from a paperbark gum, a worksheet on metaphors, even fairy floss to melt on their tongues as a writing prompt.

They still don't understand.

They get *what* the metaphor is. They don't get *why*. The poet, trudging along, eyes falling upon *bacon redness of bark…* what does it *mean*?

"It's a joyful image," I explain, "Playful."

They disagree. Most don't eat bacon, some don't eat meat at all.

"It's grotesque," Yousef, whose family fled Lebanon, declares. "The tree looks like flesh. Red, peeling flesh."

"It's a sad image," believes Muhammad from Somalia, who once told me the best thing about Australia is that you can walk to school without worrying about getting shot. "The tree reminds him he is hungry."

We're stuck on the bacon tree. Can't get past it. The entire poem's overstuffed with difficult words, convoluted images.

They understood Robert Gray's other works. The poem about the train bursting from the tunnel towards the sunlit sea. Last term's presentations contained endless stories about arriving in Australia. Stepping into blazing summer heat, warbling alien birdsong. The bittersweetness of leaving everything for a new home. And the poem about the burning rubbish dump, read under a sky orange from distant bushfires, amidst headlines about children marching against climate inaction. Our country's own pathetic, self-wrought war.

But this poem, about a moment of joy so absorbing you forget everything else…

We head outside, hoping it'll inspire something, and watch ibises pick through playground rubbish. *This part of the West,* headlines declared last week, *will eventually be too hot to live in.*

We try our hand at metaphors. Fairy floss clouds. Sun glinting off concrete like buried treasure. The air is wool-thick, restless.

I feel a sudden, impotent shame. What use is this poem to children who've faced so much? Just another white poet describing bushland that each day is devoured a little more by highways and factories.

It's a bad, flat day. The sky glows at the clouds' fringes, full of headachy, scattered light. I should give up. But it feels like a sticking point; I should be able to give them this. The bacon tree. The transcendent moment.

The sky swells, warps. Rain starts— slow, then fast, hissing against the hot concrete. At my old school the kids would've run, screaming, for cover. Here, they regard me quizzically.

"Inside, Miss?"

"Wait," I say, "This is a *sunshower.*"

Sunshower, a few repeat. Playing with the word, enjoying it. And the rain, the sharp relief of humidity breaking.

"Remember the poem?" I say. "*A quiver of rain.* The *wet light.* And he *walked, on and on, in such vibrance.*"

"What's vibrance, Miss?" someone calls.

"Energy. Something striking. Something bright."

With any other class there'd be rolled eyes. But I watch hands stretch to catch scattered drops, and their mouths, working, *sunshower, vibrance,* tasting the newness of language.

TREE CLUB

This is their tree. It rises straight from the square pit by the school's side door along a busy boulevard, then divides into three staves, which divide into branches, lifting reams of toothed leaves. According to the city certificate their tree is something called an American hop hornbeam. It belongs to them: the club's President, the Vice President, the Secretary, the Social Media Director (already snapping before pictures), a dozen other students, and, in a lesser way, the English Teacher. Tree Club.

They begin by picking cigarette butts and plastic bits out of the pit. They prod the soil with tools like birds' feet. (Like this, someone asks? The Teacher, knowing nothing about trees, says: Looks good to me.) They pour water from the can into the pit and spread a layer of mulch, red like clay.

The President reveals a sign, made that day in Art, a watercolor painting of a fluffy green tree urinating on a frowning brown smudge. It says: "Our tree wouldn't pee on your dog."

They water their tree every Tuesday, but there's not much else to do. Tree Club is bored. The President has an idea. Next week, everyone will bring a rock to line the tree pit. That way, she says, everyone will know it's ours.

Most bring rocks from parks and playgrounds, grayish and whitish rocks, anonymous rocks. The Secretary has brought a smooth cream-colored rock, like a lump of ice cream, engraved with a Chinese character, but she doesn't know what it means. A sophomore has brought a dark round stone, like an olive, from a beach in Trinidad, near where her grandfather lived.

Are you sure? The English teacher asks her. It might get lost.

But she bends down and places it carefully with the others.

By October, Tree Club has lost half its members. The President is bitter. They made a commitment, she says. The English Teacher wants to say: But that's the way it always is. Work piles up, new friends emerge, new crushes. The newspaper, the play. Some always drift away.

The leaves of their tree have turned a rich red gold, like honey in a jar. Across the street, another tree is Post-it yellow. I thought they were the same kind of tree, the Secretary says. I didn't realize they were different trees until just now. That's the way it always is, the English Teacher wants to say. In the fall, that's when you learn who everyone really is. All those colors and shades they were hiding—brassy, mellow, pale, outrageous—are suddenly, at once, revealed.

In January the Vice President plays with the cords of his hooded sweatshirt while the English Teacher reads his college essay. It's dry and dreadful. A list of awards and achievements, as lively as a press release. I think, the Teacher says, you should write about the tree.

What he means is this: I have seen you in the cold, picking trash from the tree pit with gloveless hands. Replacing the mulch. I have seen you, when snow is coming, pick grains of rock salt, one by one, from the pit. Everyone else has forgotten the tree, even the club's President, but you remembered, and I saw.

The tree, Mister? the Vice President says. It's nothing important, though. Just a tree.

After Spring Break, their tree flowers, and Tree Club is reborn. They apologize to the tree for neglecting it. They genuflect and hug it; they make gestures of penitence and reconciliation. They flush the pit with propitiatory water.

The flowers are white petals stacked into drooping tassels. They look like fish, someone says. They look like pine cones. They look like the ash on a cigarette. (The Teacher pretends not to hear this.) They look like socks. They look like cat's tails.

Those graduating make the others take an oath: I shall remain a keeper of the tree. Each puts one hand on their heart and one on the tree. The oath-takers are laughing, but in the seniors the English Teacher senses a familiar current, the future's wind, that makes them somber when they expected to be light.

And then it's done, it's summer. Tree Club adjourned.

Do I need to come back over break, the Teacher thinks, and water this thing?

Don't be stupid. The tree will be fine, will live. Watered or thirsty, mulched or unmulched, the tree will remain. The cars on the street will keep on speeding past it, desperate to get wherever they are going.

EXTENDED MELODIES

DIANE MEHTA

I worked all day, but nothing took.
Not even thought would take a look.
Not still the nothing that was me
mattered much; tuneless and multiple, free,
I kept it up, and orchestrated some ensembles—
cello, birdsong, violin; autotuned it, added cymbals
and got the curve and scaw of personality
wrong, my pitch too wide harmonically—
clatterings and shatterings. Soundings universal
escape my ears, pursuing joy, enjoying trouble.

SOMEONE BY A FROZEN LAKE

TOMAŽ ŠALAMUN

TRANSLATED FROM THE SLOVENIAN
BY BRIAN HENRY

From moment to moment
we'd grind truth and grain and

grass and coffee. And why, why?
I went through a girded

country. The fishermen slapped
columns. The sun banged,

covered up, but banged again.
Burned paper lay

in the streets. With my left
middle finger I

removed the sleep from my right
eye. I didn't stop

writing. Only now, when
I raise a glass of water.

THE SKIN OF THE ASSESSORS IS COVERED WITH BLACK FLIES

TOMAŽ ŠALAMUN

TRANSLATED FROM THE SLOVENIAN
BY BRIAN HENRY

If I had three bits of bread,
I'd toss out

the first when the train crosses
the Soča. For the second,

I'd pretend that
I forgot it on

a bench. I'd turn the third
in my hands,

raise it during the ride.
Chains are

attached to the trees.
The bread booms.

The bread breaks. Devastation
is unnatural.

WHO IS PORCELAIN

TOMAŽ ŠALAMUN

TRANSLATED FROM THE SLOVENIAN
BY BRIAN HENRY

And whoever directs the process with an open
mouth will summon a brown glass in vain.
The beans are scattered under the truck.
The opening fuels the sound. Because I'm beautiful and blue
and juicy and large. Horsehair in algae.
And who is porcelain? There's nobody here who'd
be porcelain.

BOYHOOD

NICK FLYNN

It's like a camera—if you leave
the shutter open more

time bleeds in & with it

more light, until
their voices fill the space

you remember. If I fell—
I probably did fall, I was always

falling, into onto over
something—that enormous

rock in someone's
front yard, it was the moon

& I was leaving
my footprints all over it,

it was an iceberg & I was
its doomed ship, it was

the top of a mountain, an entire
world buried below the lawn.

It was taller than a man, it had
fallen from heaven, or

a spaceship, I'd climb it
when we'd visit, once a year or

so, before I ever made it inside
that house I can't remember—

I never knew who anyone was.
I was told to say hi so I said hi.

INCANTATION FOR A LAKE

HUSSAIN AHMED

In this picture, I walked   down the steps
into a lake   dressed   for funeral
except no one I knew died   but the numbers   rose
from the right corner of the TV screen.

Before I left my room,   Baba called
asking if they would let me cross the border back home

        if they have found a field to bury all the dead,

        if they now let people warm their lovers' palms one last time

or   if they let them have their ashes.

        South of this lake,
a shepherd dog   guards a car cemetery.
        I understand
its tired eyes know   coyotes don't eat metal scraps.

        The dog would be happier
in a farm   than here,
        where every bent rim
 or cracked rearview   is proof of scars and survival.

My wrists were tied
behind my back

with a tesbihi
or guitar strings,

when I tried
     to wriggle them off, it vibrated
and the dog came running towards me.

     In a small office
packed with faulty speedometers, a man made a gun joke –
     I showed him my palms.

I surrendered my brown rosary to his mouth
     and he chewed on it, as I counted my regrets
for coming this far   away
     from the lake,   away
     from the room where I kept count
     of the dead numbers as they climbed.

I collected my regrets
like dews on the grasses   in my backyard,
where no one mowed   for months
because we were unsure where the virus bred.

MY SISTER LIKES GIRLS AND DOES NOT RETURN FOR MY MOTHER'S FIFTIETH

TAWANDA MULALU

Months after I hadn't had my first oyster
before I came to America. My sister in Canada now

where it starts snowing soon. Things I haven't seen
keep cropping up. Movies are colonialism

and I'm such a dutiful director, swerving cameras
around oceans I hadn't had before. Flying in

I'll ignore the masses of land
locking home. I'll wait for the next flood

to take us once we finish ballooning the sun
and her hot response to our earthly gassiness—

I haven't seen polar bears either yet. My sister
posts pictures of herself

swimming through snow
and the melting goes slow as it can.

Every day I wake waiting for water
as if I'm still home as if my ancestors are still

praying for something as so simple as myself
walking across the river here thinking

when. I'll jump into it in sheer drunken
blaze. My sister had graduated.

My phone's wet. My parents buzz.
The leaves are red

and falling now. Hadn't seen that
before either. I'm always surprised by rain.

AN AUTHENTIC LIFE

JENNIFER CHANG

For most of my life
I did not know or understand
the names of things
I saw every day. Sugar maple, crape myrtle.
I mistook ignorance for wonder,
wonder for grace.

As a child
I watched a friend as she rode
English style, not knowing
English was not the same as American.
It was a lesson. From a bench

I watched my friend play master,
envied her riding crop, her khaki jodhpurs.

I loved horses
only in theory,
by watching. No horses
hid in my toy chest, no lessons
my parents would've strained
to pay for.

I had not been taught to ask questions.
What is this. Who are you. Why.
I had not been taught to want.

My family was not poor,
exactly. We simply had no imagination
for pleasure.
To us, it was hard enough being American.

Pleasure, as I've learned,
is a will to knowledge. I would never,
like my friend, sit straight-backed
atop a horse. Even in Arizona,

years later, an adult,
I curled into the animal holding me,
overwhelmed.

I was riding Western style
up the side of a mountain,
the name of which I've long forgotten,

tottering over the ground, over the horse,
over the dust
scratching at my throat.

I laughed into my horse
in what I considered Western style.

When older white people speak to me
they assume I had been a child fluent
in deprivation,
that hardships were endured
to stand before them.

Do they think
she has never ridden a horse,
nor driven aimless towards the California coast,
do they think
she has not disobeyed her masters.

Once I watched others ride,
and now I was riding.
That golden memory,
the nights it took

to reach red dirt
and not even see the Grand Canyon.
Was that my deprivation?

That golden memory
of holding on and rising.

———

I read a story about a boy
who'd wounded horses at a stable.
One night, he found them
motionless in their stalls. He was
a groomer or a collector
of oddly colored stones. Torn loose
by time, he merely mistook
which animal was in captivity.
I remember thinking,

his violence had something to do with
the Latin word for horses, the noun
a crown of meaning.
What looked like equality
I deemed it so – the horse and I
sharing a kind of understanding.
The horse and I, companionate
if not comparable. Which is to say,

the horses failed the boy
for being neither human
nor wild enough.
The excess of their submission
forming an ache
he had to give expression to.

I did not ride the horse, only watched.
I was a child fluent in deprivation,
wasn't I?

Now that I think of it,
I read the story wrong.
It was not a boy
but a man in the field, and

it was not a horse
but the child of himself
standing astride,

the field relentless, tall grasses
wounding us with their ghostly braying.

What I remember
keeps happening,

the sun chasing at my back,
the chance to ride
infrequent as freedom,
everyone watching.

Piero Manzoni, *Achrome*. 1961.

ESSAY / *H. L. KIM*

RETURN MAIL

MISSED CALLS

Aren't you worried about him?
No, not really. He will be okay.

At the tone, please record your message. When you finish recording, you may hang up or press one for more options.

산소 *sanso* (noun)
1. oxygen
2. grave

1. oxygen

Grandfather, did you hear my response? Sister called me heartless for it. I cannot expect any sympathy from her. Sister's contempt was hardly enough.

Grandfather, I am sorry. I said such words without knowing that the hospital would soon call to apologize. You were dying, and they were asking for permission to give you "comfort care." Sister and I would struggle to translate this for Mother. We had never learned how to say "comfort care" in Korean. We never knew that we would need to someday.

They are Mother's familiar words when separate, "comfort" and "care."

Comfort—*how do those jeans feel, try squatting in them, would you need a belt, is the fabric soft enough.*

Care—*do your teachers check for that, make sure to pack your bag, will you buy a house for me and visit often when I am old.*

Comfort Care—*Mother, they say it will be hard for him to go across the night.*

2. grave

We did not record your message because of a bad connection, please try again. To record your message, press two.

TO PICK UP

Taped to my wall is a collection of envelopes. These envelopes have never contained letters. Because there were no letters inside, the writing is inked on the cover of these envelopes, where the recipient's name usually lies.

A friend points to the Korean writing on the envelopes. "What do these say?"

Three of these envelopes are from Grandmother and one is from Grandfather.

Grandfather's is all I have left of him now. Grandfather's handwriting is barely legible. This was one of the last things he wrote before his hands began to shake too much, unable to hold a pen. Soon, Grandfather will be moved to a senior rehabilitation center, where he will contract COVID-19 during the post-Thanksgiving 2020 wave, one week before his scheduled vaccination. He will pass away at the hospital, three days before his birthday.

Anyway, Grandfather writes that he's proud of me because of all the academic accolades I have received. I didn't realize that he was so proud because he had abandoned his dreams for an education when he was my age, as the oldest son and sole breadwinner of his family. I didn't know this until after Grandfather had died.

Grandmother's envelopes all ask if I am eating well and insist that I should eat well with the money she encloses. I didn't realize Grandmother was so insistent about food because she had fled from North Korea as a young child, begging for rice and watching siblings die of starvation. I didn't know this until we watched a movie together on the Korean War and she cried afterward. I was fourteen years old. I only understood half of her words; I wish there had been subtitles for what Grandmother said.

Where does the other half go, the half that I did not understand? I don't know, but now I understand why Grandmother always makes warm eggs and rice for me, even when I am no longer a small child. *Rich people food*, she calls it.

"What do these say?" I answer, "Oh, you know, the usual. 'I love you, stay well, we believe in you.'"

Though I grew up with Korean from the cradle, it would take me a decade to pick up Korean. But the more Korean I understand, the more obscure these envelopes become. I gather the questions into my arms and bring them to the mortuary.

Look carefully, notice how the words shiver. How the words themselves are speaking beyond their syllables. Each letter spilling a string that reaches for you, an inkling of a breeze carried, asking   *Are you on the line.*

RETURN ADDRESS
돌아간다 *doraganda* (verb)
1. to return to original state/place
2. to die, to pass away

It is time to leave. We are standing by the curbside, next to the cars that would take us home. We wait for Grandmother.

Grandmother walks toward the white chrysanthemum stand. I see her because I am reading the Korean printed on the bereavement ribbons. She holds the ribbons in her hands and turns her face away.

Dear Grandmother, you write to me in Korean but who taught you how? Mother told me that you didn't go to school, not even primary school   Dear Grandmother, for how long were you fleeing from the North into the South   what did you leave behind   when you say that you begged soldiers for rice were those NKPAs or ROKs or Americans   and who did you stay with   who was kind to you and who was not   what was your brother's name   you only had one brother and he did not make it   I do not remember who told me but I know that this is true

I know your mother survived because Mother tells me that she shared a bedroom with her   I know that one of your older sisters survived because I met her daughter but what about the rest   who do you miss   before you fled and before you feared before you were a mother and my grandmother   when you were just Daughter what is it that you dreamed of?   you like that my dream is school   Grandfather's family in Korea hated you because you never went to school   once I admired your courage   you fled from your in-laws while Uncle was growing in your stomach I was inside Mother who was not yet inside you   now you are inside me leaning on my memory   me here learning the shape of yours   your courage, leaking   I mourn how you must have kept it from leaving   my heart clenches because yours is a fist ever since   Grandmother, when you gave me your English homework what did you see   all I saw were crosswords and fill-in-the-blanks   you must have seen a little girl kneeling on carpet   fingers curled around a pen   when you stroked the girl's hands and exclaimed that she was good and smart and your pretty puppy   to whom do your hands belong to, Grandmother or another little girl the little girl over there   kneeling on dirt holding a rice bowl begging

(where does this little girl belong   who is she   has she clung to you or has she followed me   I have never met her but here she is in my memory)

in the end, Grandmother, I do not know where you were born   where you fled to   where you abandoned your fear   I am your American granddaughter so all I know is North and South   in the end I do not know how many siblings you lost how many friends you remember   how many soldiers you saw   how many homes you made   how many were left   how many nights you slept hungry   all I know is   fifty stars   two Koreas   and most importantly thirty-eight   thirty-eight the armistice   an agreement, a truce   but the number hardly agreeable nor ever true in the end   it is just like this—   the difference between twenty-six English letters twenty-four Korean letters   the two of us   Dear Grandmother, have you been told?   your penmanship is beautiful

Grandmother yanks at the ribbons, rearranging them so the black print faces the ground. (His face, under the dirt mound, faces the sky.)

Grandmother, why are you turning the ribbons over?   now they are blank   I cannot read them(Grandmother it is a relief to know how to read don't you agree?)please stop I would like to read them I know that I can now   Grandmother, turn the ribbons back   now no one will know his name   *Grandmother*

please stop pulling at the ribbons   to remember I must read them   already this
memory shakes   you see I remember my questions but not his name

FISH OUT OF WATER

기억 *giyeok* (noun)   미역 *miyeok* (noun)
1. memory   1. seaweed

Memory is a fish out of water. The fish inside the water nibbles on our hooks, the curvatures of silence and questionings. Our fishing rod never lies. To the fish, it nods in agreement and excitement. This is when we reel in the fish.

A fish out of water is not a fish but chunks and globs of seaweed. Stubborn and slimy, memory is the seaweed brewed inside our *miyeok-guk*, the savory seaweed soup consumed on birthdays and postpartum.

Miyeok-guk—Mother's recipe, remembered: water, garlic, seaweed, fish sauce. *It's easy to understand*, Mother told me, as if the soup speaks. *This, you must always remember how to cook.*

Miyeok-guk—Daughter's memory soup: black asphalt, Mother's tears. Grandfather's casket behind a wall of Plexiglass, one parking-lot funeral. One Korean funeral hymn, I remember the tune but I do not know the words. The fishy smell from Grandmother, a side effect from her new medication. Leukemia—the English word that she does not know. *Leukemia*—the Korean word that I do not know. Like the funeral hymn, I know that I heard the Korean word before because it was Google Translate that told me that Grandmother has leukemia. But I do not know the Korean words. The words to the hymn, the word for leukemia. Sometimes, Grandfather's name.

Memory likes to visit what we do not know, and what we do not know is hard to understand. What is hard to understand, we remember. Memory visits as seaweed when we remember the fish that we must have missed.

ALL YOU CAN EAT

막다 *makda* (verb)
1. to stop, to block

Mother is smart in the mother tongue. Daughter is not. Is there a daughter tongue? Could the mother tongue and daughter tongue understand each other?

I am a bad daughter because I struggle with Korean. I consumed so much English that it blocked the airflow to the mother. I am mortified to call Korean my mother tongue, my first or native language. Not when it has settled for last place, foreign in my throat.

If there were a daughter tongue, I would think it is silence.

But I refuse to reduce my Korean into a language without definition. I must have a name to call it by. To be without definition is to lack shape, to lack a weighted presence. Korean—the language I lost in the cradle, the present I waited for. I would pick it up at the cemetery.

Daughter is smart in the daughter tongue. But Mother is also a daughter. Mother is also smart in the daughter tongue. So we sit in silence, heads bowed.

I have many questions, Mother, but they are tired and rest on our silence. I don't have the heart to push, not yet. My heart still mourns the fist.

Are you hungry? Are you lonely? Are you angry? Are your feet tired from wandering? Do you know where you are? Do you have a place to sit? Would you like to sit here with me?

먹다 *mukda* (verb)

1. to eat

When Grandmother feeds me warm eggs and rice, she feeds all of her siblings who never grew up to taste warm eggs and rice at a marble kitchen table. Grandmother is Catholic, so I suppose it is wrong to say that she is feeding ghosts.

They follow me wherever I go, and sometimes I let them see through my eyes and think through my mind. I do not know what to call them.

Do you understand me? I am late to arrive at our language but I am here. Are you there? Is there a way I can call for you when I do not know your names?

They emerge, these almost-ghosts, nearly visible but not quite, every time I make cold buckwheat noodles, *mul-nengmyun*— the style traditionally eaten in the northern region of the peninsula (before it was called the capital-N North by the Americans). Translates directly into "water buckwheat noodles" because the broth is cool and clear like chilled water. Perfect for a hot summer day.

They watch me place dried buckwheat noodles into a pot. I direct my sight to the stove, the faucet, the electric cooker, the *mul-nengmyun* broth packets. A tube of mustard, one hard-boiled egg. *Don't worry*, I say to the almost-ghosts. *There's plenty, I promise. We will all be fed.*

WHAT'S IN A NAME?

묻다 *mutda* (verb)
1. —
2. to bury

묻다 *munda* (verb)
1. —
2. to swallow

It's silly to call it grief, sillier to call it by any other name. Silliest to call it nothing. But those who grieve need no naming. After his passing and after my leaving, my throat assumes that I have given myself a new name. I'm fine, it says most. One hard syllable, easy to catch and quick to be heard. Light to carry, simple to believe and to remember. To swallow grief like one swallows pride or anger, breath abated. Why do I not correct my throat? Perhaps it believes my old name died, buried with the man who gave it to me.

물어 *muro* (verb, imperative of mutda)
1. ask

물어 *muro* (verb, imperative of munda)
1. bite

With every passing day, grief awakes a new metaphor. The way grief is an ocean, a forest, a sky clear and cloudy, a chair emptied. The way memory and silence become the same. Grief, a fishing hook dropped into the ocean, asking for a bite and a response. The question mark left for silence's taking. Grief becomes birthday soup at a funeral. A blank letter paper inside an empty envelope.

The paper is imaginary. The envelope is real. Grief is the misspelled name on the envelope. The one letter removed changes everything. Grief erases similes and smiles. Nothing likes grief, nothing like grief.

But you must name your grief so it listens to you.

Daughter faces grief. Grief is the envelope with nothing inside. Grief is the letter she will not find. Grief, the letter never returned. A pile of empty envelopes with no place to go, no return address.

You must name your grief so the letters can find you and stay—twenty-six English, twenty-four Korean, the two between us.

Grief is the pen held in a hand. The knuckles bend, a gentler fist. They grab another envelope, reading   *I hope this letter finds you*

Piero Manzoni, *Achrome*. 1962.

FICTION / KRISTIN KEEGAN

SNAPSHOT

Conflict erupts across the street in the two-story house whose white paint has weathered into sizable gray smudges, the thumbprints of a giant. The lawn of this house is neglected, half-dead, edged by three Italian cypresses that are surviving but not looking happy about it. The conflict seems to be this: the mother (thin, hunched, a cancer survivor) has locked the adult son (thin, hunched, an alcoholic) out of the house. He pounds on the door with his fist, words of half-hearted menace slurring from his mouth, and when no response comes from within—no answering voice, no door opening—he strides into the yard to call the cops.

This is the point at which I reach for my notebook and pen. Clues might be forthcoming, and indeed are. An overview is given to the dispatcher: He was locked out because he was petting the dog (her dog, evidently, not his). His meds are in the house (sedatives, antidepressants?). He pays to live there (disability, SSI?), and she has no right. *"No right!"* He gets emotional. The call gets disconnected. He hits 911 again and accuses the dispatcher of not caring. He answers a few questions then gives his cell-phone number, which I jot in my notebook.

Of course, the dispatcher knows him. All the cops in town know him. They are summoned to this house on a regular basis, arriving in two squad cars usually, often accompanied by a fire truck or an ambulance. On ambulance days he puts up no resistance and strolls unescorted to the gurney, where he stretches out and gazes at the sky. Is there a dash of eagerness in his surrender? He displays no reluctance to transition to whatever existence the gurney offers. Nor do I detect resignation (certainly not the grim resignation of the three Italian cypresses, with their pursed, dark branches and in-held sighs). Perhaps this is because when he is taken away, it is never for long. Often he returns later the same day in a taxi, which parks in front of my house.

A German boyfriend I had decades ago, an arborist, told me that Italian cypresses reminded him of exclamation points, an image I enjoyed at the time and have continued to savor since. Cypresses often appear in cemeteries—well, hardly *appear*, as they have been purposefully planted to form a boundary, just as they do in this neighborhood. I've thought about Fritz's (not his real name) image: exclaiming cypresses! In cemeteries. Not much exclaims in a cemetery— this treespeak could be a message for the living that shouldn't go unheeded.

Today the police, who have arrived in two squad cars, are not taking my neighbor anywhere. He rants awhile, clearly intoxicated. They soothe, the door gets opened, and then, the situation defused, they leave. When he vanishes into the house's spectral interior, I wonder if he gets to pet the dog.

All this I witness from the upstairs window of my house across the street. Most of it, anyway. A Monterey pine has sprung up in my front yard, flinging green shade across my windows, and though I've toyed with the notion of removing it, I have not. Why? Perhaps because it is a problem child, deserving of a more tender approach. This child was unplanned—some joker of a breeze tossed an eager seed into a fertile patch of dirt in my front yard. Monterey pines once did very well here. When this neighborhood was developed fifty years ago, these trees were all the rage and hundreds of them were planted. But, like so many things in life, what is a darling one day becomes a disaster the next, and today the trees are a bane, weakened by drought and subject to infestation by bark beetles. All over the neighborhood (and town and state) Monterey pines have died, are dying, or will die. (But why do I go on so about trees? You probably think I can't see the forest for the trees.) In any case, I adopted the little upstart, and while I have not nurtured it, still it has shot up, hale and hearty, and now it is lanky enough to block part of my view of the shenanigans at the house across the street. Its way of thanking me, I suppose.

I don't mean to make light of my neighbors' difficulties. They suffer, this pair, caught in hard circumstances. There was a daughter, too, but she is gone now, having flung three blue Samsonite suitcases into the back of her pickup and roared off. I puzzled over those suitcases. They were stylish but dated and looked barely used. The daughter may have returned once or twice, moving back and then leaving again, I don't know. It is not my job to monitor this family's every move, though I do keep notes.

Any detective worth her salt would suspect that something more is going on across the street, more than cancer and alcoholism and the unruliness of modern life. But that's always the case, isn't it? We get only a glimpse, and glimpses can be misleading. It's like the insipid board game my kids enjoyed playing ages ago—Snapshot, it was called, a catchy enough name, though I believe the game promised more than it delivered. In this game, a plastic grid of little hinged windows covers a black-and-white photograph, and players take turns choosing which window to open—what in the world? At any point the cockier players can throw out a guess. It was somewhat fun, I suppose, though I always lost. Forest for the trees, right?

Recently I came across this game in the garage and was startled to see the box indicate the game is for ages six to sixty, so I would no longer be eligible to play. Perhaps I should be relieved rather than outraged.

Sitting at my window now: the light is fading, early or late, I don't know. Daylight saving time just ended. I detest DST. If you rearrange the letters you have *DTs*, the clinical abbreviation for delirium tremens. There is a kind of delirium in thinking we can tamper with time, which of course is only our notion of time, something we've concocted to chop up our days into manageable bites. The house across the street grows silent, bewildered. I think this house wonders where it is, and no streetlights have blinked on yet to help orient it. I could wonder what's going on inside (rants or pleas or inebriated slumber), but I will watch the sun exit instead. Pressing closer to the window, I see it creep away, wearing topaz slippers and dragging a cape of fizzling embers. I watch until it is gone. Then conflicts are put away, notebook closed, pen capped. *The Mystery of the House Across the Street* is tucked in for the night, an early bedtime. I hope it stays put.

I've decided those Italian cypresses across the street aren't just surviving but are bullies. They are a muscular gang, nudging shoulders with the clouds, looking for a fight. But clouds are the wrong target today, bulky but timid, quick to scamper away.

Neighbors are unseen today, unheard. I'll call them Fern and Devon. Those aren't their real names, which I know but won't disclose. But Fern and Devon are close to the real names. Cousins, I would say.

Once, I offered to take Devon to an AA meeting. I'd recently retired (there's a clue about me), and I suppose I was looking for a charitable project, albeit a small one. Devon came from across the street when he saw me hauling boxes of Christmas decorations to the garage. He surveyed my garage with a bemused shake of his head and then offered to help organize it. From what I could judge, he wasn't drunk but wasn't completely sober either. It was midmorning. I thought him sincere in his offer but did not even contemplate accepting it, imagining the wreckage that might ensue. True, wreckage had already ensued in my garage, a junkscape of boxes, shelves, furniture, and filing cabinets topped with a strata of papers, clothing, toys, picture frames, and picnicware (when was my last picnic?). I resented the Christmas boxes, resented their cheerful contents—Styrofoam snowmen; construction-paper Santas; gaudy ornaments crafted by pudgy, sticky fingers—and every year I considered a purge. Once, years ago, when I was in therapy, my counselor, a divorcée who saw clients in a cottage behind her home in a location I won't reveal, broached the topic of clutter. She was an effusive woman—her chattiness was probably intended to put me at ease—and she told me how she, too, had accumulated tons of stuff from her children's school years but at some point realized she didn't want *that crap* (her words) and hauled it all out to the dumpster. I was shocked, aghast, but part of me admired the stand she'd taken, the sacrifice she'd made. I think it was a sacrifice.

It's not that I don't want my kids' stuff. But I'm only its custodian, keeping it until such time as the kids want it. Then I'll unload it, and they can share these artifacts with their own precious children, *ooh*ing and *aah*ing over Santa's faded pinkish cap and his lumpy cotton-ball beard. If they ever have children, that is. If they ever have spouses. (The latter condition no longer necessary for the former, of course.)

My children's names will not be disclosed. Nor will aliases be offered.

But you're probably wondering what progress I made with my therapist. Of course, I wasn't just seeing her because I had too much stuff in my garage. There was mental stuff, too. Baggage. (Flash to three blue Samsonite suitcases in the back of a pickup.)

Progress was made. Accomplished, wrought.

How tedious it is to talk about one's therapy.

But Devon's offer. Did I tell you he is gay? He told me this once, told me how difficult high school had been for him. He'd tried to start some sort of gay alliance, a club or something, but the school offered little support. This would have been decades ago when everyone's thinking was narrower.

Gay is a Christmassy word, isn't it? *Don we now our gay apparel.* Devon's apparel wasn't gay, however, that morning in my garage. He was unwashed, dressed in a grayish T-shirt, faded pajama bottoms, and flip-flops. He has ginger coloring, and his appearance lacks firmness, definition. He meant to be kind, I could see that, and perhaps he wanted to be connected as well. Did he see me as some sort of maternal figure, someone who might offer something his own mother could not? I have no idea. I don't think of myself as maternal. Yes, children have drifted through my life, just as Devon will, but I don't cling to their roles or to my own. I don't even like the word *maternal*. It sounds so bloated and preposterous, especially when partnered with *paternal*, a far saner and more judicious label. But I knew he would soon wander off, back into the smudged house across the street. I've never been inside their house. Once I examined it on Google Maps, an aerial view, and was surprised to discover an in-ground swimming pool in the backyard. The water looked inviting, an optimistic turquoise, but who knows when that view was captured. It's not like you're peering through binoculars at the present moment. Today the pool is probably empty, or if it has any water at all, its color is a murky olive green.

Technology can be useful when solving mysteries, but of course it wasn't always so. Years ago I shared with my daughter (yes, one child was a girl) a series of Nancy Drew mysteries, the original ones from the 1930s, which I'd tracked down and purchased on eBay. During my own girlhood, I'd discovered these same small volumes on a dusty shelf in a corner of a library in a small Midwestern town. Even then the books were dated, with their blue cloth covers, quaint illustrations, and tallow-colored pages. Daughter and I started with the first story: *The Secret of the Old Clock*. I enjoyed the book more than Daughter, who might have been too young to fully appreciate Nancy, that quick, resourceful girl left to her own devices. In the original illustrations of the 1930s she's sketched in clothes that would hamper sleuthing: long tight pencil skirts, impossibly high-heeled pumps, and a dashing hat of some sort, a beret or a flirty little Robin Hood number. Dear Nancy, a flawless creation with her high spirits and her roadster.

That January day with Devon in my garage—or it might have been a February day, truth be told, since I seldom get the holiday crap returned to the garage in a timely manner—that winter day (though winter in northern California is probably not what you're picturing, unless you live here), I asked Devon about his drinking. Oh, I know, the time to discuss drinking with an alcoholic is not when they're inebriated or even tipsy, but you have to seize opportunities when they arise. Devon knew of an AA group nearby. He said he'd attended once or twice. It seemed doable—driving him there, waiting for him in the parking lot, driving him home. I suppose the spirit of Christmas was still ringing in my heart, nudging me toward the betterment of mankind. Or maybe it had something to do with my birch tree dying (another casualty of the drought) and Devon volunteering to help cut it down. Can you imagine me handing him the chainsaw? So, two things he'd offered me, garage tidying and birch cutting, and I offered only one: a lift to an AA meeting. And I couldn't be much more than a driver, certainly not a mentor or a sponsor or even a sober friend. I was, after all, barely an acquaintance.

He took my number, then jokingly asked, "Should I call you Mary?" which I didn't get at first, until I realized he didn't know my name. I could have gone with Mary (responsible for Christmas, after all) but instead gave him my real name. It seemed harmless enough. He hasn't called. He knows where to find me. And now I have his phone number too, since he shouted it at the 911 dispatcher for all the world to hear.

I'll call the therapist Alyce (not her real name, though the affected spelling is similar). I saw her for several years. She dressed in trendy clothes, flowing garments in earth tones accompanied by long scarves and dangly earrings. (Nancy wouldn't be caught dead in those clothes.) I remember Alyce's clothes more than any insights or advice she offered. I think I ended up knowing more of her story than she knew of mine. Something tragic happened to her as a child— mother and father killed in a plane crash. I still think of that sometimes, Alyce as a little girl being told such news. The moment when a life veers off course, careens into the unexpected. Though such a moment bears thinking about, it is difficult to contemplate for long.

Have I been neglecting the mystery, the fragmented snapshot of the house across the street? I'm still trying to get a sense of it, take it in, examine its edges. I don't have a name for it. It's a miasma (no edges then), questions and unknowns and *whys*. Its color is gray, but not sedate gray. No, it's shadowy, disturbing, lingering.

I'm not young, which is not to say I'm old, even though my hair is mostly gray and there's jiggle fat under my arms and my chin has acquired an underling. My skin is as lined as notebook paper, which isn't at all the right simile since my lines are not straight but bent and wavering. And of course they're not printed lines, though I do believe they were stamped upon me in some way (the stampede of years galloping over me). Well, we all age, don't we? Or meet the alternative in some shocking, unexpected fashion (plane crash possibly).

She hasn't aged, our youthful, sleuthful Nancy. Her detective work spanned decades, but she never matured much. And why should she? Yet change did come, though not by her volition.

I could say more about aging, the changes time brings to the body, to the psyche, but my words would not be original, and I doubt you would learn anything new. If you're curious about this process, simply look around, there's plenty of us out there creaking along, galumphing about, looking faded, washed-out. Washed-up too, many of us.

That's not such a bad image, is it? *Washed-up* suggests something unexpected cast upon a remote stretch of beach. Oh, I know, in detective novels it's always a corpse or a wrecked motorboat or the wing of an airplane, something disastrous. But the washed-up thing could just as well be lovely: a pinkish fluted shell or an emerald ring (without a finger attached!) or a glass bottle with a message tucked inside. And don't we elders all have messages inside, carefully penned (in cursive even), carefully rolled, just waiting to be discovered and acted upon?

What would my message say? (Quick, call Alyce to explore this! But no, Alyce of the Sedona sunset swirls belongs to the past.) My message should be something profound, encouraging, life-sustaining. But what comes to mind is a different sort of message: "Help! I'm being held prisoner! Save me please!"

If Nancy found this washed-up bottle bouncing along the tide line, what would she do? First of all, she'd give the case an alluring title: *The Clue in the Old Green Bottle. The Mystery of Half-Moon Cove. The Case of the Missing Matron.* Though that last title is hardly alluring. *Matron* is an ugly word, clunky as stilts, and who wants to read a book about an old lady?

Perhaps she scans the beach for further clues, but her discerning eye finds no evidence of anything untoward. Then her sleuthing skills kick in, and she begins an interrogation.

"Who are you?"

Easier to say who I was.

"Based on your penmanship and the distraught content of your message, I'm guessing you're a woman," she would say. "Describe yourself."

Gray.

"Can you be more forthcoming, miss? Which particular mayhem has befallen you? Robbery? Kidnapping? An assault upon your person?"

None of these.

"Have you misplaced something precious?"

My mind perhaps.

"This is no time for wry prevarication! What kind of jam are you in?"

I believe I was taken prisoner, though not by brutes, goons, or hoodlums. It's all rather murky. I think I'm a victim, but I might just be a witness.

She puzzles over this. "I suspect you're ensnared in some sort of lurking abstraction. Drat, that's the worst! Can you describe your whereabouts?"

A house. With windows.

Already she is adjusting her cloche and sprinting toward her roadster. "Sit tight, I'm coming for you!"

I'd be most grateful. But Nancy . . . ?

"Yes, miss?"

You need to be careful. You're the one in danger.

Tossing her head, she laughs. "Danger!"

But you don't know what awaits you—there's a certain kind of peril reserved for plucky girls like you—

"I can take care of myself!" Then, revving the engine, she hesitates. "About your bottled-up message. If you're going to rewrite it, you might include something about time. After all, my very first case was about a clock with a secret."

Something about time's disquieting nature, you mean?

"How should I know? I'm only in my teens, and I'll stay that way forever!" She gives me a smile and then tears off in her machine, top down. Maybe she is a model for how time should be faced: with shoulders squared and a saucy tilt of the head.

She would label my case *The Mystery of the Missing Woman in Gray*.

Gray again.

How I ramble about. (Add that to creaking and galumphing.)

Do you know what happened to Nancy? Those early books gave no hint of the disaster that would befall her, though there was a certain recklessness in the way she drove her roadster. But her circumstances were favorable: Despite having been left motherless at an early age (no explanation), she was well cared for by her father, Carson (wise, measured, an attorney), and their housekeeper, Hannah Gruen (plump and slightly dense). They resided elegantly in River

Heights. The old editions are treasures because at some point in the 1950s the publisher decided to rein Nancy in. This girl who'd flashed through caper after caper in the thirties and forties, this bold, impetuous girl who enjoyed "complete freedom" with her "keen mind, a quick sympathy for those in trouble, and an ability to look out for herself," our Nancy, well, she underwent an editorial lobotomy. She became less outspoken and more demure, less independent and more accepting of help from others. The books were rewritten to showcase this newly shackled Nancy.

I'm not saying these books, in their original format, represent great literature. The writer's hand is often heavy. Carolyn Keene (a pseudonym, definitely not her real name) loved the pairing of speech tags and adverbs: "chortled boisterously," "demanded incredulously," "returned grandly," "suggested nervously." One male character goes so far as to "disclose his chagrin." But what these books represent (grandly) is a passage to another world, and isn't that what the best books do? The titles alone invite the reader on what promises to be an unforgettable journey. Who wouldn't want to join Nancy in visiting Lilac Inn, Larkspur Lane, Shadow Ranch, Red Gate Farm? Who wouldn't want to witness a whispering statue or find a clue in a broken locket?

Well, I go on. Either you like her or you don't. But if you're inclined to go looking for her, search for the original Nancy, the one who was "always impatient for action."

I'm back at my upstairs window. The Monterey pine jumps about in the midday sun. I think this tree is far too vibrant for bark beetles to be feasting upon its innards. Its arms and legs splay against the bright air, cheerful and confident, at home in this world. I peer past it to the house across the street. No signs of life. Did I mention their blinds are always closed? (Obviously mine are not.)

Sometimes I wonder how ill Fern is. I only know about the cancer because I saw her body grow thin and her hair disappear, replaced by head wraps. I sense her hiding within her baggy clothes as she goes from her car to her front door, not wanting to be seen. Not just by me, but by anyone in this whole suburban world. I don't blame her—it's a strange place here. Once, on the phone with a friend (unnamed), I misspoke and said "suburgan" instead of "suburban." Carolyn Keene would probably tag this "blurted impulsively," but, really, I misspoke due to a kind of swaying muddlement caused by a second glass of zin with supper. Anyway, I found myself warming to the notion of living in a sub-berg (however you want to spell it), a submerged iceberg where all is hidden, treacherous. It is like that at times, our world of similar homes, similar yards, similar schedules. A *bedroom community* it is called, with most residents away at work all day. Those of us who do not work only venture out in the midday, when it's easier to get about. But once it's time for bed we are all back here, present and accounted for.

And yet, despite our similar trappings, we are all so different, aren't we? We remain unknown to one another. But here's a conundrum—if I don't know my neighbors, how do I know they are different from me? I don't know Fern and Devon, even though they've lived across the street from me for twenty years. I watch, I witness, I speculate. But I don't know. We all have our depths, an unseen region where the essence of who we are is held in pristine glacial complexity. Or maybe it isn't pristine—maybe it's marred with striations of petrified wooly mammoth dung. More speculation. I know so little about any of this. Any of us.

And I've boldly labeled it treacherous, this suburgan world, but that's probably only because of the *Titanic* (menacing iceberg rearing its head to rip open a ship of oblivious souls). I'm not suggesting such deliberate menace occurs here.

So, I don't know Fern and Devon (though I suspect they would have been stuffed in steerage with me, fancy suitcases or not). And nobody knows much about me. I don't reveal my spindly hopes, my tampered dreams. I could share more, but who's really interested? I'm not saying that with regret ("cried piteously"). I have my circle of friends, my contacts. And family of course.

I haven't mentioned Ned, Nancy's boyfriend. Her fellow. He's another story. We've all had our Neds, haven't we? Alyce's files must be stuffed to the gills with agonizing references to them. Ned is a good enough guy, I think, but I don't want Nancy to marry him. She'll give up too much or have it snatched away. They've already done a hatchet job on her, those ghostwriters and editors and publishers. She can't lose much more of herself.

Action again, outside the house across the street. The front door opens. Devon slides out. I lean toward the window, taking it in. Devon seems about to disclose his chagrin. Then I see Fern coming out too. They wander toward the cypresses. They're not together, but not exactly apart either. Will they speak to each other?

I could reach for my notebook and pen, but I don't. It's enough for now, this glimpse. I'll leave them there on the withered lawn, leave them to whatever words will come, whatever actions will unfurl. It isn't my business, and it's almost lunchtime, which I've already planned—a bowl of vegetable soup, a handful of oyster crackers, a slice of salami foiled by a cup of turmeric ginger tea. I'll eat this on my back patio, away from the trees, sitting in full sun. Exposed, and maybe waiting.

Piero Manzoni, *Achrome.* 1960.

HEAVEN

One of my earliest memories is of my grandfather burning paper offerings so that my grandmother would have a comfortable afterlife.

First, he burned her a house—a simple, three-room construction that stretched the full width of my six-year-old wingspan. Then, he burned her food: paper cutouts painted to resemble the tenderest cuts of meat, juicy cabbages, jewels of exotic fruit too expensive to eat in life. Next, he burned paper money. "Now she can go shopping in heaven," he said. His word—*heaven*.

When I told my mother this memory, she slapped me across the mouth.

"That was me," she told me. "I was the child. I told you this memory, and now you've taken it for your own, you selfish girl."

That was decades ago.

When my husband, Dongshen, died, I didn't burn him any joss paper, even though we each grew up in villages where people burned paper effigies of meat and fruit more frequently than they were able to eat them.

He was not always a kind husband, but I did not derive any perverse joy from depriving him in the afterlife.

He was just pragmatic, as was I. It would have been a waste.

So I am surprised, then, when I receive an email from a woman claiming to have been his churchmate in Harbin.

I'm eating alone in my usual booth, halfway through a buffet plate of fried chicken and flounder fillet drowned in starchy sauce, when I receive it. I swipe it open, scan it once, then again.

I might have deleted it, except they used his full name, the one he gave up after we moved to America.

And something rang off, or true.

———

Dongshen did not believe in God. When we met, in college in Beijing, we were both devout atheists. Each of us had been ranked number one in our hometowns, earning a university seat in the nation's capital. After a decade of fourteen-hour days spent studying textbooks by candlelight, it was hard to believe in anything beyond the small, concrete objects that lay in front of us: wood, paper, ink, lead, and stone.

When we first moved to Texas, a neighbor invited us to her church and Dongshen laughed when I accepted.

My only experience of religion was from my childhood, when the police raided an underground church in our village. So I was awed when the neighbor drove us into the parking lot of what seemed like a huge stadium.

"You know what they worship?" my mother told me when those Christians were arrested. "They think heaven is an endless buffet where you don't get fat and you don't get full. Lazy." She scowled, her cracked teeth gleaming, then spit into the gutter. "Lazy, stupid," she repeated. "So lazy."

I agreed with her then, a daughter's habit. It wasn't until years later that I perceived the sweetness of this idea of heaven.

My husband died three months ago.

He was out there for hours before someone found him. I'd already gone to bed. When I first got the call, a little jolt burning through my half-sleep, I thought, *a joke*, probably one of Christopher's or Katie's friends prank calling, and then a sick, sinking feeling as I remembered both of my children were grown, had their own jobs and lives in cities far away from this one, felt my stomach drop as no punch line came, no snickering laugh, not even a cough—just that fat, unwavering silence, thick as a body, on the other line.

"Are you sure?"

My body shook, and I felt very light, almost pleasantly so. I thought it would play out like a movie, like in one of those crime-scene dramas: Dongshen's body cold in a drawer, pulled out, a devastating wound in his chest.

Reality was simpler: they had me come down to the medical examiner's office—that is where they had taken him instead of the hospital, already dead when found—where a plump, tired woman led me down a long hallway into a small windowless room. On a worn, clunky desktop computer she clicked through photographs one by one: Dongshen's body from the chest up; a close shot of his face; then an even closer shot of the birthmark on his right elbow.

"Is this your husband?" the woman asked.

I recognized the jowl lines instantly, the distinct balding pattern on his scalp. It was a shock to see him in photograph and be unable to touch him or ask for an explanation. He looked—I reached for something less cliché but could think only of this word—calm. The only indicator that he'd been mortally struck was a deep, swelling bruise across the left side of his body.

"Are there photos of where you found him?" I asked. And the woman nodded.

"Are you sure you want to see?"

I believed I was. But when she clicked to the next photo, I looked away.

It was only later, in the car driving home, wearing a T-shirt too thin for the night's chill, that I thought again of Christopher and Katie. What could I say?

When I arrive home from the buffet, Christopher and Katie are in the kitchen, putting away groceries. They are earlier than I expected.

It is the second week of February, and my children have insisted on visiting—whether for Valentine's Day, that nonsense holiday of cartoon love, or because I've announced that I plan to go through Dongshen's things this weekend, I'm not sure.

Christopher must have driven down this morning. He lives a three-hour drive from here in a city in Texas that's bigger and more expensive than this one, the one Dongshen and I chose over thirty years ago for the schools. Katie must have taken a car from the airport after her red-eye. That's sixty dollars. When she goes back for her return flight, it will be another sixty dollars.

From behind the open refrigerator door Katie meets my gaze, her eyes swollen and red.

Katie never tried to hide her emotions. Even as a child she often cried, snot-nosed, into Dongshen's shoulder. At first he was tender, but as she grew older and her troubles grew—the anorexia in high school and the intensive outpatient program she went to for it; the year of college she spent at home, recovering from what her college dean called "clinical depression"—he became tougher, less forgiving. "There are people with real problems," he said once. "And you are not one of them."

Now, she sniffles as she crosses the room, a grocery bag still twisted in her hand. She hugs me, and I can feel her ribs.

"Mommy," she calls me. "Mommy, how are you doing?"

I look at Katie's shoes—these expensive calfskin boots she asked me to buy her two winters ago, during her year home.

"You went grocery shopping?" I ask.

"I did," Christopher says. "Just on my way here."

"You didn't have to do that."

"Where were you?"

"Running errands. How was the drive?"

"Long, the usual."

My mother, who is dead, used to say that I would never understand her until I had children of my own.

I thought she meant that motherhood would refine me, invoke the kind of supreme, selfless love the other women I knew cooed about when they first became mothers. Often, at night, holding Christopher's small body above bathwater or watching Katie asleep in her crib, I was instead struck by their density—the meat of their bodies grown inside then cleaved from mine, just as mine had grown inside my mother's—and I imagined how I must have looked to my own mother all those times at the wooden table, a hungry three- then seven- then fourteen-year-old, and I looked at my own children, so solid and happily discrete, who had been born on hospital sheets stiff with bleach, the fluorescent lights so clean and white it hurt to look up, a kind of violent purity, and quick, hot rage rose in my throat like bile.

It was in those moments that I came closest to understanding my mother.

"Mom, are you listening?"

I look up. "I miss him, too." But even as I say it, and even though tears leak down my face, it feels like a betrayal.

"I'm going up to work," Chris announces, taking a bottle of seltzer—a kind I've never seen before—from the fridge.

Christopher is always working. He does a job that I don't understand and that he has never tried to explain. He discussed it with Dongshen, though—Dongshen was always into business. When the kids were younger, he tried to start his own investment firm in China.

I remember driving to Good Fortune Supermarket to refill the calling card, how we tracked the time to the second, twenty-seven cents a minute. "I'm so close," he said. "I think we could have something big."

"Please come home," I whispered. The kids were asleep in the living room—we hadn't yet moved into a house, didn't have any real furniture.

Eventually, he did come home, took an engineering job at a company with a whole office park full of cubicles, just like me, just like all of us, a sea of PhDs with accents and faces like ours. Sometimes I think about that period of my life and marvel at how strong I was, how capable. I don't think I will ever be that woman again.

That night I make dinner—something easy and beloved from when they were younger. The email from the woman in Harbin pricks at the back of my mind, but I push it away and instead focus on slicing ginger paper-thin, carefully trimming the coarse fat and hair from the meat and rinsing it with boiling water to get rid of the scum, remembering the way their faces used to light up when the smell wafted out from the kitchen, how all three of them lapped bowl after bowl, like puppies.

But when he enters the kitchen, Christopher grimaces. "I actually stopped eating white rice," he explains. Katie, too, has cut out simple carbs and meat. I look at her again, closely this time, checking for signs, but she seems solid, no trembling of the hands, her skin a healthy, tanned color. I stare at the congee I made—white rice, chicken, and ginger simmered soft, topped with flecks of dried pork and preserved egg, a delicacy.

"It's okay, Mom," Katie says. "I was going to have a smoothie anyways."

Already, Christopher is at the fridge, pulling out a tub of salad, the family-sized pack of grilled chicken breasts he must have bought at Costco. The price tag says $17.99. The meat looks rubbery, cartoonish. He piles two onto a plate, then lifts a breast to his mouth with his hands and begins to chew as he adds salad to his plate. He's already finished with the first breast by the time he's sat down to eat.

Though I usually eat once on buffet days, I pour a bowl of congee for myself, and together we eat.

"We should start with the bedroom closet," Christopher says between mouthfuls, "then move to the hallway closet." He had arrived with a list.

———

After dinner I clean up, put everything back in its rightful place, burn away all residue of our eating with chemical disinfectants that come in bright, cheerful bottles.

The pot of congee is body-warm, comforting to touch. I hug the pot to my stomach. If I wanted to, I could eat this entire pot and everything would be almost the same as now.

I take one bite, then spit it out and throw the rest of it into the trash. All I can hear is my mother, her voice a harsh whisper: *The waste, the waste of it all.*

I shower, scrub at myself under the armpits and groin until I can no longer smell any meat, emerge raw and new.

In the dark of my bedroom, I stare into the white screen and pull up the email. There it is, just as it was.

From: yfeitom184@qqmail.com
Subject: 谢东昇

Hello, my Dear,

We heard of your loss, we are regretful it happened and wish to offer our sincere condolences to you. Recently, the world is very difficult, but your husband was a light in the darkness, he added so much to our congregation. In our service last weekend, we sang a song in his honor, I attached it here for you to see.

If you want, you may add me on WeChat: NxVD091081.
I hope I have the right contact information.

Sincerely,
Jenny

Despite the implied promise of a recording, there is no attachment. I wonder if this is a sincere error or merely a scam—does she want me to write back?

When I enter the ID into WeChat, a message appears: *User Not Found.* I try different iterations, thinking there might have been a typo, then google the email address and username. Nothing meaningful comes up.

———

"Welcome, welcome," everyone said when I first visited our neighbor's church. "Jesus loves you." A fountain glittered and sprayed water, surrounded by flowers. We entered the worship hall, and it was unlike anything I'd ever seen—bigger, even, than the university hall where Dongshen and I received our diplomas. They all stood up to sing—there might have been a thousand people in the audience—and I recalled those Christians in my hometown, lined up at the edge of the wet, open gutter where chicken blood mixed with oil mixed with grass and hair, always so much hair, where children defecated wildly, singing even as an officer handcuffed them then loaded them one by one into the back of a truck.

I couldn't help myself. I opened my mouth and sang, too.

Dongshen's sister Li Ping arrives the next morning with a box of candy hearts and several folded-up cardboard boxes. She lives alone in a sprawling house that is a forty-minute drive away, her husband having moved back to China years ago to live with his younger mistress—an open secret we all pretend not to know. Her son lives even farther out from here, in pharmacy school.

"My dear sister," she cries when I open the door, wagging the candy hearts in my face. "Happy Valentine's Day!" Her positivity has always bordered on denial.

I make a note to throw out the candy later—perhaps I can leave it on a park bench somewhere so it doesn't go to waste—and accept the cardboard Li Ping is now pressing into my arms. "I saved these from Johnathan's move," she says. "I knew they would come in handy one day."

I haven't touched Dongshen's things since he died, and I feel afraid, suddenly, seeing all his things laid out. I didn't realize there'd be so much. I tell Christopher and Katie to separate what they want to keep. Then, although I feel the futility of the question even before I ask it, I pull Li Ping outside.

"Did Dongshen ever say anything about believing in God?"

"What?"

"Or a church? In China?"

"Where in China?"

"Harbin?"

"In Harbin?" she repeats, shaking her head. "No, I can't think of anything. Why?" I tell her about the strange email. She seems relieved to know as little as possible. "These internet scammers are so cunning now," she says. "Really sophisticated. My friend, her hairdresser's son got scammed out of his life savings. They started talking and he fell in love, and next thing you know, she told him she was kidnapped, that she needed fifteen thousand dollars ASAP or she would be killed. And he loved her, you know."

"Maybe, but this doesn't feel quite like that."

"Just be careful," Li Ping says.

Li Ping heads to the bedroom, where Katie and Christopher are folding sweaters, and I begin laying Dongshen's shoes out in the foyer—twenty pairs of running shoes alone.

I thought Dongshen and I would grow old together, that he, like me, would give up the fight against his body's soft formlessness.

Instead, in middle age, Dongshen became enthralled with exercise. He started reading books on eating for your body type and going on 5 A.M. jogs. "The hardest part is starting," he told me. "But once you do, you unlock something in your mind that was holding your physical body back."

In the dim bedroom I shared with my husband, I glance over at the piles my children have created—Christopher has chosen a few workout T-shirts, and Katie has picked out just one sweater and a T-shirt. I thought they would take more.

"Chris, you don't want any of these suits?" I ask, impatient.

"No."

"You don't even want to try it on?"

"This kind of suit is expensive. I think this one is from Dillard's, look: Made in Italy," Li Ping offers.

I remember when I bought it. Dongshen had just returned from China, had just started applying for jobs. The saleswoman spoke to me in clipped, beautiful English. When I pulled out my credit card, her eyes gleamed.

"I just don't wear that kind of stuff," Christopher explains, eyeing the pile of clothing.

"Fine, fine, I guess it's just trash."

"Don't be like that, Mom," he says, putting an arm around my shoulder.

"You don't even want any of his running shoes?"

"I have enough running shoes."

"I'll take some shoes, and a suit, for Johnathan," Li Ping offers again.

It's too much.

I'm in the foyer, then the front doorway, keys in my pocket, waving a quick *see you later*.

"I have to go, I forgot, I had this errand to run," I say, rushing, rushing. Then I'm sealed quick into the car, and then I'm off, driving to where I don't know, except I do, an impulse deeper than anything.

When I return home, Li Ping is gone. Everyone is sympathetic. Christopher has added a suit and two pairs of running shoes to his pile, and Katie is wearing one of Dongshen's sweaters. It hangs down to her knees. That was one of his nicest sweaters—the last time he wore it was to a dinner party Christopher had been invited to for Columbia students and their parents. I remember driving to the other side of town, how the house had its own lake. How the other parents, eyeing us, praised the excellent golf courses in Singapore. *That country is so clean and modern, isn't it amazing what they've accomplished?* How, before we left, I had the impulse to take a bottle of water, though I didn't, afraid to look greedy.

They've packed Dongshen's clothes into the boxes, which they've stacked in the garage. "You can keep them for a little while," Christopher explains, "and decide later what you want to do with them."

"Thank you."

"Mom, are you okay?" Katie asks.

"Who said you needed to ask if I was okay?"

"You look tired and sick," Christopher says.

"Thank you."

"No, we mean it," Katie says now. "We are worried about you."

"I know all this stuff is hard," Christopher says. "Do you want me to stay here for a while?"

"And what, risk your job? No, I'm fine. Li Ping A-yi checks on me. And I have friends."

"You could visit New York," Katie says. "You can stay with me."

"And what. Sleep on your couch? I am an old woman. And besides, I have work."

"I can sleep on the couch and you can sleep in my bed."

"Don't be ridiculous," I say. "You'll lose sleep and then you'll be bad at your job and get fired. And then who will pay your expensive NYC rent?"

"Mom," she says, exasperated.

"I am fine," I snap.

What I want to say: I own a house. I own a car. I have two children, a boy and a girl. I eat meat three times a week. I have a closet full of clothes I never wear.

That night, Christopher insists on taking us out to a nice dinner for Valentine's Day. The building is valet parking only—I watch him hand the man a twenty-dollar bill.

Inside, brass chandeliers hang from industrial beams painted matte black; the walls are tiled with intricate mosaics of wood, which the hostess explains come from a special forest in Japan. It's loud and crowded, the tables set so close together that the hostess must slide the table out for me and Katie to sit down. She hands us three menus—thick, velvet backing—each: specials, drinks, food. There are no prices.

"You've been here before?" I ask Christopher.

"Actually, this is the first time I've been able to get a reservation." My children beam, studying the menus, already at ease.

A waiter comes by to take drink orders and explain the specials, but I can barely hear him over the other voices in the restaurant. Their conversation could shatter glass.

Christopher orders for us—a string of words and phrases I barely understand, they sound more like textures and colors than food. Someone brings three teacups of tea that tastes like rice.

"What do you think?" Christopher asks. "Isn't it nice?"

"It's nice," I admit.

The food begins to arrive—tiny cubes of it, exquisitely arranged. Everything comes in enormous ceramic bowls, which are cartoonishly large compared to the food.

"Oh, wow. Wow, wow, wow." Katie snaps photos as every course arrives, Christopher waiting patiently for her to finish before he portions it out. They give me the best portions of everything— two oysters, a thick slice of wagyu, the first and biggest scoop of a dish that I later learn is called "egg on egg on egg" (soft-boiled egg, uni, roe).

"Excuse me," I ask the waiter, pointing to the egg dish. "But just out of curiosity, how much is that dish?"

"Mom!" Katie says, giggling.

The waiter laughs. "That's okay. This particular dish I believe is seventy-eight dollars. It's got the uni and caviar on there, as well as that fresh truffle."

Seventy-eight dollars. That's more than four weekday lunch buffets, tax included.

I hate to admit it, but the food is good, better than anything. At the buffet, the things I eat are soft and starchy, salt and garlic and onion. But here, each bite is nuanced, delicate. I suck an oyster from its shell, and sweetish brine gives way to something tart and jewellike—pomegranate seeds.

The food awakens something in me, an old hunger, and I am afraid, then, of how much I want and how badly I need. I finish everything in front of me, then look up at my children, who are still working on their plates. "Are we still hungry?" I ask. "Do we need to get more?" Already, I'm envisioning fat steak between my teeth, crusty bread dipped in its juices.

Katie eyes me warily. "I'm full, but you can have the rest of my plate," she offers. Has she eaten enough? I am ashamed of how terribly I want to reach over and plop those juicy fragments into my mouth—to take food from my own child.

"We can order more if you want," Christopher says.

"Oh, no, no, I was just thinking, wondering, if you two had had enough." I smile. "I'm full." My stomach is a blank stone. When the bill comes, I look away.

In the car on the way home, strapped into the passenger seat as Christopher drives, all I can think about is soft donuts, fried chicken, frozen cheesecake with thick graham-cracker crust.

At home, Christopher and Katie disperse to their rooms—already I can hear the hum of their laptops, the intro music for a popular television show Katie likes about a beautiful, young, white mother whose wealthy parents cut her off when she has a baby out of wedlock.

I search the kitchen for something like what I'm craving—doughy, sweet, fried—but there is nothing, my pantry kept intentionally bare. I could go to a drive-thru, but how would I explain my absence? I could make a rudimentary dough from water, egg, and flour, then fry it, but then the whole house would stink of it, and my children would wonder, *Why? Why? Why are you frying homemade dough in the kitchen at 10 P.M. on a Saturday after we just ate a three-hundred-dollar dinner?*

I drink a glass of water. I count five seconds, then ten, then thirty, then a whole minute. I set a timer for ten minutes and tell myself that if I can survive for that long without eating anything, I won't need any more food tonight.

I last the ten minutes, but that night I can barely sleep. I've just managed to finally doze off when a buzz surfaces me from my thin sleep—a notification.

Hi, my Dear,

Did you read my previous message?
    I wrote my WeChat wrong last time, my apologies. This is my correct one: feitomato1981

Jenny

I type the ID into WeChat, then hit *Send Request*. It is accepted immediately. I click on the username, then hit *Call*.

A voice, hesitant. "Hello?"

I scramble up, not knowing how to approach. "Um."

"Hello?" the voice repeats. "Hello?"

Finally, I manage "How did you know Dongshen?"

My voice rings loud, and I rush outside then without thinking, not even perceiving, really, the dawn's bright cold, focused only on trying to catch every word from the voice on the other end of the line.

The woman explains that her English is not very good, and I switch to Mandarin. She gasps audibly when I tell her I am Dongshen's wife, and when I ask why, she says that Dongshen told everyone I was American, that I didn't speak Chinese.

"Are you?" she asks now.

"Yes, I'm American," I tell her.

"Oh," she sounds doubtful, disappointed. "But your accent is so good, so Beijing."

"I'm taking lessons."

"Oh, well…"

"How did you know my husband?" I ask again, this time nakedly impatient.

"He was a founding member of our church," she says, hesitantly. "About twenty years ago. He brought us Bibles and hymnbooks from the US."

"Why?"

"It's technically illegal for us to worship, we can't get—" the woman explains, but I cut her off.

"No, I mean, why are you contacting me?"

She pauses, and I hear her breath. She could be forty, thirty, twenty years old, a teenager for all I know. How strange, I think, that she could be so far away—half a world, entire oceans—and yet her voice right up in my ear.

"We just wanted, I guess, to send our condolences. He was a big part of our lives."

"I see."

"And we're not just a church, we have a center for migrant workers' children, too. We feed them, give them classes. For many of them, that's their only meal of the day."

Do I detect a sudden slyness in her voice? Was she involved with Dongshen? Is this all some elaborate scam to extract money from a grieving widow?

In my left hand is the box of candy hearts from Li Ping—I must have grabbed them instinctively. I open the box and pour a few into my mouth.

"Sounds like important work," I say, not bothering to mask the sound of my chewing.

"Not yet. I mean it is important, but until we have more resources, it's hard to really change anything."

I grunt, still chewing, allowing the different flavors to mix on my tongue.

"I heard you sing beautifully," she offers. "Dongshen said you were a professional. If you ever visit Harbin, I hope you'll consider coming to sing in our church. The children would love it, they never—"

"Who do you think you are?" That quick rage again, rushing up.

"I'm sorry?"

"Contacting a grieving widow to drag up old memories."

"I didn't mean to upset you, I'm so sorry. We thought it would be nice, we were hoping—"

The candy is brute sugar on my tongue, bald and sweet. I chew, swallow, eat another handful as she continues her apology, then eat another, until the box is empty. I walk as I eat, allowing the hand holding my phone to drift further and further from my ear until the sound of her voice dwindles, then disappears.

I let the empty box drop to the ground. I smell wet leaves, hint of fertilizer and dog shit, residue of motor oil; something warm and laundry-scented wafts from a house nearby. I look down and see I'm wearing a pair of Dongshen's running shoes.

I haven't paid attention to my walking, but I now realize I've been heading toward where Dongshen was struck. I never actually went to see the place where he died, but Christopher and Katie did.

Christopher insisted on flowers, a little cross—"Not religious," the saleswoman explained to us, "just a symbol of love for the dead"—placed at the side of the road. If it had been up to me, I wouldn't have wasted money on something so tacky.

I don't want to see it now, but still, I find myself walking toward it. I brace myself for that cross, but it's not there when I arrive. At first I wonder if I've gotten it wrong, but when I reach the place—unremarkable, just an ordinary intersection, it could have been any place, except it was here, this place, where it happened—I feel it, a shift, and I know.

Dongshen died alone on the side of the road. It was a clear, warm night. His blood shone on the concrete. It leaked into the gutters.

I'm not sure how long I stay there, watching the morning approach, then thicken, but then it is morning. Just down the road is a cafeteria-style restaurant with a weekend breakfast buffet.

I could go back to get my car, but I might have to face my children, explain where I am and where I am going. It's a twenty-seven-minute walk, just over a mile, which doesn't seem very bad at all.

The route leads me down several neighborhood streets, then an alleyway, then the pedestrian walkway bordering a busy road, which opens onto an overgrown field alongside the highway. I've forgotten how unfriendly Texas is to pedestrians—how impossible those first years were with no car. The field is muddy and thick with burrs, dry bush snatching at my ankles. On the other side—just another fifteen minutes, the map says—is the restaurant.

By the time I arrive, my pants and shoes are caked in mud, my forehead sticky with sweat. "Just one," I tell the hostess. "For the breakfast buffet."

"Um." She pauses, then seemingly decides, for she lifts her chin up and smiles wide. "Right this way, please."

After she seats me, I go to the bathroom, wash my hands and face, then rinse my shoes in the sink. I wet a paper towel and dab at my pants, rolling them up at the ankles.

At the buffet, I hold my breath. I'm early enough that everything is newly laid out, pristine. Buttery eggs, waffles, French toast, layers of bacon and, in a smaller tray beside it, a mound of tiny pork sausages.

I am thinking of Dongshen, who never had an appetite, never understood what I meant when I said I was craving meat. I am thinking about my mother, who quickened to rage when I said I was still hungry as a child, I who had never known famine, who never ate tree bark, boiled the leather off her shoes. That terrible hunger and that terrible fullness.

I eat one plate, a second, a third. Then, I go to the restroom, pretending to fix my hair in the mirror while I wait for it to clear out.

I eat again, then again I go. Then again.

Over and over, I feel eyes on me, watchful. But every time I look out, nobody is actually looking.

The truth is, after I visited our neighbor's church that first time, I kept going back. Always alone.

I'd mostly stopped after college—the habit was more than I could afford, even if I did mostly do it on rice and salt—but the church invoked something in me that day, its shining lights and surfaces, its message of forgiveness and everlasting life. Being there made me feel like I could become the woman I'd always intended to be.

I liked the church. I liked the way everyone smiled at me, how I got to park in a special spot because, technically, I was still a visitor.

I liked the free coffee, which I drowned in hazelnut creamer, and the free donuts and kolaches, which I ate in quick, huge bites.

I liked how, at any time, I could close my eyes and pretend to pray.

I liked the handicapped bathroom on the second floor, next to the elevators. I liked how it came up so easily, in neat, doughy bites.

I never did it when I was pregnant. I'm proud of that. As far as I know, nobody ever saw me.

I never let it get too far.

———

I saw Dongshen just once.

It was late at night, and I awoke from a bad dream, sweating. Dongshen wasn't in bed. I rose to find him, but he wasn't in the living room or the kitchen, nor his office. I began to panic, but I crept upstairs quietly—Christopher and Katie were sleeping—and found Dongshen sitting on a beanbag in the guest room, faced away from the open doorway. He was watching something on his phone.

At first I couldn't make out what he was watching, it was just writhing shapes of light, neutral and pallid. But then it came into focus and I saw three men, naked and hairless, twisting together on a bed. They looked almost like young boys, that's how soft and hairless they were, the three of them twisting together in one long, undulating river. It was dark, but in the illumination of the phone screen on Dongshen's skin, I saw the flickering outline of his wrist and thumb, curving up and down his own penis. His head cocked in devotion.

I perceived then how a person could be at once so specific and so unknowable.

I would never know Dongshen, no matter how many nights I slept next to him. He—his appetites and desires, his experiences of the world—would remain unknowable to me forever, and I to him.

It was the same with our children. They had been conceived and grown inside my body, but once born, they took on an irreversible difference, one of outsidedness, and became something else—many things, in fact, all unknowable to me.

I think about this now as I stare into the toilet bowl, wipe threads of sour spit from my chin. I flush a final time, wipe the seat down, then check the underside. I emerge, spit, rinse, scrub.

I look up, and the restaurant has grown crowded, families lined up for the waffle bar, groups of college students drinking mimosas. I become aware then of my state—disheveled, muddy, cold— and prepare to leave, but I don't have a wallet.

I'm frantic, searching every pocket, even the lining of my underwear, for something, anything, and when I look up, Christopher is there, a terrible look on his face. He does not look at the pile of dirty plates scattered with bones, a stack of bowls with the oily residue of soup, cups of soft serve and cereal, a single spoon.

"I tracked your phone here," he says, blankly. And it's not at all how I thought his voice would sound.

"Mom, Mom!" Katie cries when I get home, running down the stairs to hug me. I'm terrified I smell, but I let her hug me anyways, this daughter who is so, so small in my arms yet so vibrant, who, even at her sickest, knew enough to stop when full, or before that. She's just showered, her hair wet, its wetness seeps into my shirt. Somehow, beneath layers of perfume and body cream and shampoo and laundry detergent, she still smells like milk to me.

Later that afternoon, Christopher will knock on my door. That night, he will drive the three hours back.

Katie will fly out early tomorrow morning before the sun is fully up. Who knows when we will all be together again, sleeping and eating under one roof?

He tells me he and Katie are planning to visit Dongshen's grave that day, and would I like to come too? I'm so tired, I tell him, and he is warm, understanding. They've each brought a letter to read, he says. We've had the conversation before, but again he wants to know if there's anything I can tell him about his father, if there were any last words.

"I'm just"

And what can I tell him?

That my mother slaughtered pigs for a living? How, when I found her, she still smelled of it, pig shit under her fingernails.

About the summer Dongshen spent at the quarry, breaking rocks the size of cars down into smaller pieces. A pallet of loose, stacked yellow granite sold for a thousand yuan—a month's work. The way his hands blistered and burned.

About the time, before him, before any of this, I was supposed to have another child, but it leaked it out of me after just three months. The way Dongshen's parents blamed me. That Dongshen snored at night, that I found his breath so repulsive, wet on the pillowcase, that I started sleeping in Katie's room after she went to college? That we hadn't had sex in nearly two years. That, when he'd first started running, he'd tried to get me to go with him, and when I couldn't keep up, he said Katie was lazy because I was lazy.

Hello, my Dear…

"He was preparing for a marathon," I tell him. "He said he loved you and Katie very much."

Did Dongshen go to church?
And if so, did he sing?

During our first year in America, Dongshen took me to an all-you-can-eat Korean BBQ buffet, and I looked at the piles of meat and wept. At the time, he thought it was because I'd never seen such excess—that I was happy. In truth, I don't know why I wept, but know only that it was not happiness or relief that flooded me. I felt greedy that day, eating, gleeful. We avoided the rice and vegetables to make more room for the meat.

The night before my mother died, I dreamed of her. I was fourteen. The week before, I had bled on her sheets for the first time and she beat me, but then she showed me how to wrap myself, fed me soup made from red dates and brown sugar, a luxury.

In the dream, she was a ghost visiting from heaven. I had long, black hair down to my waist. They used to make us cut it up to our ears for school—a distraction.

"宝贝," my mother said. It is the only time I have been called this endearment. "It's even better than they said," she told me, plucking a kernel of corn from between her teeth. She took my hair into her hands. "Your hair is beautiful," she said.

"Thank you."

"You get it from your dad," she said. "He had thick, black hair, too. He was always trying to grow it out. But the guards wouldn't let him."

I nodded.

"But you need to take better care of it," she said, running her fingers through my tangled ends. "You can make a mask of oil and egg—a half cup of oil to one egg yolk, some honey if you have it, and apply it to your head, starting at the ends of your hair—that's the part that's been dead the longest."

"Okay."

"And your skin—you should drink more ginseng, and eat—"

When I woke, my scalp tingled and my body ached. It was raining heavily. I couldn't remember what it was that she'd told me to eat.

———

Is there a heaven? And if so, what is there to eat?

If I had known Dongshen would die that night, would I have asked him about God?

Like many people, I like to imagine my ideal self—a good woman, serving a well-balanced dinner, clearing the dishes in a swift and unnoticeable way.

If I had known a year before, maybe I would have started running, trained up to his level.

If I had known a month before, maybe I would have taken us on vacation somewhere. Nothing too expensive—he wouldn't like that. But something nice. Like a three-star hotel. A place with a bathtub and a view of water.

If I had known a day before, I would have cleaned the kitchen so that he could wake to a clean house. He made coffee that morning in a dirty kitchen. The pot is still there, a ring of mold across the surface. I'd like to think that I would have been generous and forgiving. A good wife. A good woman. I'd like to think that I would have prepared, gone out to buy paper money, a pair of running shoes, a small bed so he could sleep well on his first night. Next, I would have gone to the grocery store and gotten all the fruits that were too expensive to eat in our youth. Fresh figs and dragon fruit, green plums, mangosteen, Buddha's head. At home, I would cut them delicately, trim the skin and cores, pick out seeds. I would take out the fancy plates and fruit forks—little silver ones, with jeweled pineapples on top, the ones we never used. I would make a pot of chrysanthemum tea.

I would bring it all out on a tray. He would be on the couch, unsure. He would be wearing something normal—his old shorts, an oversized T-shirt Christopher got in middle school. I would see the muscle beneath it all. He had a good body. I would have on something normal, too, though a little nicer than usual. I wouldn't want to give it away.

Later, there would be things to burn. But not yet. *Not yet.*

"Here," I would say. "Sit with me a while. Eat."

Piero Manzoni, *Achrome.* 1961.

FELLOW / INDYA FINCH

SHOTGUN CALYPSO

We were on our way from Huntsville to Houston to pick up Lonnie because it was Saturday, and it seemed like every Saturday we were dragging our asses to River Oaks, wearing shoes without holes like we were going to church. Sometimes, if Mrs. Vanessa was out of town for work, we'd stay the night with him and build a blanket fort in the unaired guest room with the plain white crib in the corner. Today he wanted to come over to barbecue. As if someone had asked him to do that, as if we wanted to pretend we liked his tasteless meat.

I rode shotgun whenever Lonnie wasn't around. When it was just us, Ma let me put my feet on the dash if they didn't leave any marks on the windshield. She didn't want to clean them off, and despite my own insistence on being uncivilized, the least I could do was pretend like I wasn't so people wouldn't call her an unfit mother. I don't think of myself as wild—wearing shoes just isn't my thing.

I was trying to enjoy the last moments of the front seat and outstretched legs before Lonnie blocked my view and leaned his seat back against my knees. Clio was laid out on the stained back seat, etching cuss words into the fabric before dragging her hand across to erase them. Ma was singing along to "End of the Road," by Boyz II Men, which meant she was about to start babbling about the time she got invited to their after-party in '94. Michael, the bass, could've been my father, and she almost named me Michelle instead of Calypso. There were other options. Daddy liked Diana, but Ma spared me a lifetime of being called Dirty Diana, and she told him Billie Jean and Annie were out of the question too. In the one college class she ever took, they read the *Odyssey* and she decided right then that's who I was. Why wouldn't she want a goddess that men feared for a daughter? My birthright was women who trapped love and took it by force even when men cried—even when they couldn't afford to stay one more minute they stayed eight more years. She'd told me these stories a million times, but I didn't ever stop laughing or gasping when the moment was right. I didn't know what else to do.

On another day the music would've been cut lower, and the three of us would've been talking about the new man we saw coming out of Ms. Winnie's apartment and our pride at her still pulling men at the age of seventy, but that day Clio and Ma were still mad at each other. For the billionth time Clio had complained that I always got to ride up front, and for the billionth time I said she could sit in the front when her birthday came before mine. Instead of accepting as she had done so many times before that her lot in life as my younger sister is to take the things I don't want, she got mad. She reached her hands around the seat and gripped both of my cheeks and dug her nails in. Clio always went for my face, always scratching me as hard as she could. When we were younger and would fight, Ma would make us both put on one of Daddy's oversized shirts he left behind and hug underneath it. Clio would grab the skin at my sides and pinch and scratch me until I bled, and I hugged her like I was supposed to. I wanted to cry, but I never did because if Ma saw tears she made us stay in the shirt longer.

Ma didn't pull over, but she did slam on the brakes, and the tires screamed like she'd peeled off their skin. Ma pulled her arm back and hit Clio in the mouth so hard her bottom lip burst open and bled. She didn't even whimper. Her face scrunched up into a Raisinet of squinty almond eyes and purple lips, and she smacked them even though she knew Ma hated that, and Ma popped the other side. She didn't mean anything by it, and neither did Clio. It was just their way. They're so much like each other. Clio's lip healed. She has a crescent-moon-shaped scar there now, but she doesn't remember from what. The car was mostly quiet as we drove up I-45.

Ma never hit us in front of Lonnie. He didn't agree that children needed to feel pain to learn how to behave. If Ma wanted to hurt him she would ask him where he got off giving advice when he didn't have any children he could point to. But she didn't want to hurt him often. Even though Ma said he was a trick, like all the men she courted, she used some restraint.

That didn't mean she wouldn't give us a look that said she'd cataloged our poor behavior and we weren't getting off scot-free. Once on a school night we made a trip to Lonnie's. It got late as we waited for he and Ma to come out from his room, and by the sound of things we knew they were almost done. We passed the time by carving butterflies into the legs of his table. It had been Clio's idea. Later we learned it was a table his grandfather brought back from the war. Lonnie never said which war, but from what Ma says, some brown family generations later were still eating on the floor. Even though Clio was mostly responsible, we got whooped together. Ma says all the time that it hurts her more than us, but I think that's bullshit. We're the ones with welts trying to hold back tears so she doesn't give us something to cry about.

Lonnie wasn't forever. We all knew that. But I think she loved him. In the way you can love a rich married man who pays your rent when you're short. Which is why we hated to have to spend so much time with him: Ma didn't need our help convincing Lonnie to stick around. If we could've stayed home with our neighbor Ms. Denise, we would have. She made butter beans to die for, we rode bikes and raced through the neighborhood with her son Cameron, trying our hardest to keep the fastest-on-the-block title. She would watch us from the stoop of her apartment, drooling, and leaning on the rail for support.

But Ma had a fear of the three of us dying separately, so we went where she went. Sleeping on the floor of the carpeted conference room or late at night helping her sweep the busted tile of the gas station and filling the beer coolers with ice so we could get home quicker.

I always wanted him to at least offer to sit in the back when he rode with us. He was the grown-up, so I know Ma never would've let him, but I hated how he could just change everything without even knowing that when we were alone, the three of us, we had different rules, different traditions. He never thought he was disrupting, and I wished he knew he was. We'd squish ourselves into the back seat, whispering to each other even though we saw Ma cast her suspicion through the rearview mirror. Every time Lonnie fell down into the passenger's seat, we watched him while he checked his teeth in the passenger mirror, ran a hand through his hair, and put his seat back so far he could look out our windows. I think it's because he thought it'd make him look slimmer, and his belly wouldn't protrude so much from between the straps of his seatbelt. Or maybe he just didn't want to be seen leaving his place in a car with chipped paint that always took a few tries of starting before the engine turned over, with a nappy-headed woman and her nappy-headed kids. I hate the way people stare, as if it isn't embarrassing enough we can't afford to fix everything wrong with our Chevy at once to make it run like it's supposed to, but they gotta let us know they see how poor we are.

He made sure to humiliate us in public too. If we were at the grocery store, he cracked stupid jokes the cashier didn't laugh at, he blew his nose into a handkerchief he stuffed right back into his pocket, and he wore white socks that went halfway up his calf. And whenever he got in the car with us, he smelled like cigars and cinnamon. Me and Clio couldn't stand it. We'd all but cover our noses with our T-shirts because Ma didn't like to roll the windows down when Lonnie rode with us. She said it'd be a waste of her perfume, the one she got at the dollar store. And even though that sugary cotton-candy scent clawed at her throat, made her sneeze three times when she sprayed it, she wasn't in the habit of spending dollars recklessly, she was gonna to make sure he noticed she put it on.

I never looked forward to that change. When Ma stopped being my Ma and became someone's lady.

I looked over at her and saw the sun shining on her face, her red lipstick, her left leg kicked up onto the seat, and the sparkle of the small diamond necklace he got her for her birthday. A big semitruck rambled up beside us. Ma tried to slow down to get out of his way, but the red-faced man in the car behind us started honking as soon as he saw brake lights. So we kept driving next to it while she mumbled a curse on his family pets. She wanted them to contract worms and shit all over his house.

"I hope he has a white carpet."

I looked at Clio through the side-view mirror and tried to get her to laugh at Ma's fantasy of a shit-covered home, but she didn't. She just stared at me and didn't let me in her head.

The truck driver was hunched with one arm slung over the steering wheel.

"Oh, Ma! Can I do the thing?" I tapped her arm, and she shrugged it off.

"What if you would've made me swerve into traffic and kill us all? And you know I don't like to be touched."

I looked at her.

"I don't care, Calypso. Do it."

Clio moved over to the passenger side window and we gestured frantically, pulling on imaginary horns until he noticed. He brought his V-shaped fingers up to his mouth and wiggled his tongue up and down.

Ma saw and honked her horn. He snapped back to the road with a little less boredom in his posture.

"What's that mean?" Clio asked.

"It's disgusting is what it is. Men are disgusting, don't ever forget that," Ma said.

"What about Mr. Lonnie?" I asked.

"He's a man, ain't he? Roll your window down."

I complied, and she handed me her lukewarm coffee.

"Throw it."

We hit a pothole and the coffee jumped ship. It ran down my hands and onto my ironed pants that smelled like I had left the heat on them too long.

"Throw it," she said again. I peeled the lid off and tossed it at the semi. It splashed all over the shiny red coat of the truck. Ma sped up to pull into another lane as he rolled his window down to shout.

"That's not fair, I wanna throw something!" Clio shouted.

"Hurry up and do it!"

Clio settled on her half-eaten sandwich that we packed from home. The soggy wheat bread slapped against the windshield. He turned the wipers on, melted cheese and bologna grease smeared across the glass. He probably could barely see. I didn't know if mustard could stain glass like it could clothes, but I still hoped it washed off soon after. Car washes are bad places. We found a body in one once, and the woman from 911 said Ma should do mouth-to-mouth, but Ma said no because the woman was already blue and stiff. I doubted the truck could even fit in one of the brick stalls. He'd have to climb up and scrape the congealed cheese with his hands and get it under his fingernails, and he'd remember us and feel hate, especially if he found a body too.

We turned into Lonnie's bougie neighborhood, the kind the Obamas could live in and the rest of the neighbors, Lonnie included, would love and adore them, but they would whisper about the maintenance of the lawn and complain about how many strange cars were parked around whenever the Obamas threw a party. River Oaks was full of cookie-cutter houses that all looked the exact same, with identical neighborhood watch and homeowners' association posts stuck into the ground. Ma wants a house someday. Our landlord stands outside the kitchen window sometimes, and we have to act like he's not there. She's tired of renting. I hope she never gets a house like these. I like columns. If we ever have money someday, I want her to buy one with columns, and I want it to be different from everyone else's on the block.

Clio sat up and pressed her nose against the window, her breath frosting in pointed arrows on the glass.

"Pirates, ye be warned," Clio said.

"The fuck did you just say?" Ma asked.

"Nothing."

"Don't get smart."

Clio rolled her eyes.

"Do it again," Ma said.

Me and Clio looked at each other.

"Why she always tripping?"

"I don't think she knows she ain't always got to be crazy," Clio thought.

Ma smacked my leg. "You know I can't stand when you do that." She looked at Clio in the rearview mirror.

"Do what?" I asked.

"You know what. Y'all get on my last nerves talking above my head," she said.

She hit the brakes a little too hard at the stop sign and stuck her arm out to catch me, but the seat belt was faster and snapped me back when my body lurched forward. Someone had tagged the sign with *Get Fucked*. I had never thought about getting fucked before. Seemed like from what Ma said, it was never something you got, more that you gave, and always felt like taking back as soon as you handed it over. Cause these boys out *here*, she would say, wouldn't ever really know what they were doing. So why bother with it, Caly? Just be a lesbo, at least then your pussy will get ate, and that's half the battle won.

The paint was still fresh, beads of it still dripping doing their best to dry. I always thought graffiti was cool. Conceptually, I mean. When I look at it too long, especially if it's chaotic and too many words, my brain starts to hurt a little. But I thought the boys, probably boys, who did it were brave in a way. Except of course that they were in the suburbs and probably put their half-used paint cans back in the garage when they were done. We took a left onto Panther Paw, the houses like perfect rows of multicolored teeth. Ma slid a glance at the white people sitting outside on their porch swing. They swirled the little umbrellas in their tea glasses by touching them every couple of seconds to make them rotate in the other direction, faces puckered at the smoke billowing from our tailpipe. Ma won't admit this, but white people make her nervous. She almost can't control herself when she's around them because she's too busy thinking about what they're thinking. Ma didn't like white men normally. She said Black men were the only real type of men she had any eye for, but Lonnie was built sturdy and had a charming smile. And what wouldn't you do for a good smile?

One of Lonnie's neighbors knelt in his yard, measuring the height of the grass with a ruler, while a young man covered in sweat waited to hear what the owner thought of his mowing skills. We stopped at Lonnie's door. I unbuckled my seat belt and clambered into the back seat; Ma slapped my backside the whole time.

"I told you to stop climbing over like that!"

I fell onto Clio, and we stifled our giggles and struggled to sit upright. Ma honked the horn, and out sauntered Lonnie. He had just gotten off work;

he was still in his blue button-down shirt, black slacks, and brown loafers. Me and Clio didn't know much about Lonnie, or Mrs. Vanessa for that matter, but we knew they must not have loved each other for a long time, that their marriage had been over well before Ma, even if neither one of them wanted to do anything about that fact. And we knew he must not have had a mother, or sisters, or really any other kind of family. If anybody cared about him, they would've taught him not to wear brown shoes with black pants.

He held a cold Pretty Lady in his left hand. He leaned into the passenger-side window, and Ma tried to give him a kiss.

"You're a little early," he said as he bopped her nose instead. "Vanessa's still here. She should be finished packing in about fifteen more minutes. Circle the neighborhood a few times. I'll call when you can come inside."

"We're not coming inside. Just tell her your friend is here and you're going to go. I don't wanna drive around till she's gone," Ma said.

In the back seat the two of us sat boring holes in his cheeks. He winked.

"Hey, girls."

We mumbled a greeting, and Ma cut us with a sharp eyebrow raised halfway up her forehead.

"*Try again,*" Ma thought.

"Hey Mr. Lonnie. How are you?" I asked.

"Can't complain, sweetheart. I missed y'all."

He stuck his arm through the window and pinched my cheek. His fingers were damp and sticky with some of the Pretty Lady he must've spilled on his hand from the walk across the lawn. He left it there, and I wanted to wipe my face but I knew how it'd look if I did. I also knew I'd have a pimple in a few days. My skin was too sensitive for his bullshit. No one ever tells you how bad puberty is. Ma told me I was becoming a woman, but if all it took to be a woman was oily skin I should've been worth about three or four then.

"I want you to come inside," he said.

"For what?" Ma asked.

"I've got something for you," Lonnie said.

"Oh yeah?" Ma asked.

"Yeah, and the girls too."

"For us?" Clio asked. She sounded skeptical, but I knew she was intrigued. Clio was a hard person: she didn't like most people, sometimes I wasn't even sure if she liked me. She was mostly mean and sometimes funny. She got that from Ma. But if she didn't fuck with you, she didn't fuck with you. The only way to change that was to give her money or a gift. She got that from Ma too.

We did three circles around the neighborhood, and after Ma saw that Mrs. Vanessa's car was still parked in the driveway she drove us to the nearby playground. She didn't let us get out because she didn't want to have to wrangle us up again and couldn't we just be patient for once.

Ma leaned against the hood of the car while she chain-smoked. She wasn't gonna be able to sneak any more until we got home and Lonnie was watching TV with us. So she crammed one in for now, the car ride home, and before they started drinking for the night.

I missed her old guy Charlie. He was fun. And he didn't have all the rules that Lonnie came with. We couldn't spend the night unless Vanessa was out of town, he couldn't spend more than $500 from their joint account on us at once, none of us were allowed to go into their room or touch her things, holidays were a hard no. Vanessa didn't ever want to be put into a situation where she had to look at us, but if they ever crossed paths he couldn't touch Ma in front of her. Lonnie had to vacuum after we'd been there so that she wouldn't find our hair everywhere. Charlie could be with us whenever he wanted to; he took us to amusement parks, he used to tell knock-knock jokes, and I'd tell him some too. He used to laugh really hard. Ma said that he was faking. I didn't think so, though. I think he thought they were funny, even though most of them I got from Laffy Taffy wrappers and Popsicle sticks. Some of them I made up. Those were the ones he liked the most.

Knock knock.

Who's there?

Calypso.

Calypso who?

How many Calypsos do you know?

Lonnie never felt like the kind of guy I could tell jokes to.

There were a million reasons to dislike Lonnie and his house, but the doorbell was high on the list. When you rang it, it played a song we always heard in church.

"For still our ancient foe," Clio sang.

"Doth seek to work us woe," I finished.

Lonnie opened the door and kissed my mother full on her lips. Ma nudged our heads past the two of them and pushed us into the foyer. He had taste. I couldn't explain in those artsy terms what style anything in his house was, but he had a foyer. When he and Ma would fuck, me and Clio'd warble at the high ceilings and it would catch our voices and they were beautiful.

Clio blew past me, clutching her purse strap between her fingers as she made a beeline for the bathroom. I skipped behind her. Ma and Lonnie were giggling like the cool kids did in the parking lot at school.

I shut and locked the bathroom door behind me. Clio was already on her knees, digging in the cabinet underneath the sink. She pulled out six rolls of toilet paper, and this was not just any toilet paper. This was the fifteen-dollar, multiple-ply, lavender-scented toilet paper. The good stuff.

I opened the floor vent and waited for her to finish sliding the cardboard out from inside the rolls before she tossed them to me. I ripped the cardboard into small pieces and stuffed them inside the vent. I fiddled with the fan switch and made sure no pieces flew past the open slats. We were always careful to cover our tracks. We couldn't use the trash can—too obvious—and we could have held on to them but we needed every inch of space we could get.

Clio set the rolls neatly in her purse with space in between each one. I opened the medicine cabinet while Clio opened Daddy's old Crown Royal drawstring pouch. We grabbed different bottles of pills and dropped a few of each into it. We squished the pouch inside a roll of toilet paper. After enough visits out here, we'd figured out how to minimize the rattling of stolen goods. Inside toilet paper was soundproof.

Clio popped open an empty travel-size mouthwash, poured some of their tall bottle of Listerine into it, and spilled some on the counter. I wiped it with one of their decorative hand towels, and we refilled the bottle back up with water, the concoction a little less blue than before.

"That it?" Clio asked.

"I think Ma said to grab her some tampons."

We opened drawers and grabbed little extras. Tiny bottles of lotions and a bar or two of soap. The tampons were in the bottom drawer; we took half the box and left some loose ones rolling around on the inside.

"You think she wants any of this?" Clio pawed through a drawer full of mascaras, eyeliners, lipsticks, and eyeshadow palettes.

"Does Ma wear makeup?"

I picked a tube of lipstick labeled British Red. "You think this would look good on me?"

"Lipstick can't fix all that," she said while drawing big circles around my moon face with her hands.

"Fuck you."

"I'm telling!" Clio tried to run out, but I grabbed her by her wrist and we tumbled to the hardwood floor. Shock ran up my elbow to my shoulder.

"I take it back!" I squealed, but that was not enough of a surrender for her. She jammed her fingers in my nose, her sharp little shovels scratching the inside.

"Say uncle!" she demanded.

I would've died instead. Though Clio was younger by a year, I never felt like the older sister, especially in moments like these. I slipped the cap off the lipstick and painted broad strokes of red on her face. She screeched as if it had been a sword. She crawled backward, sputtering and spitting the whole way.

"Why would you put this on me? They make these out of aborted babies!"

"Who told you that?" I asked.

"Minnie."

"Minnie Fischer? Minnie Fischer wasn't even allowed to watch *The Little Mermaid* with us cause her folks said it was unholy. She don't know nothing. And she always smells like cat pee."

Clio calmed down. "Most Baptists do," she said. I grabbed a wipe and approached slowly. Clio looked at me like a wounded deer, ready to flee if need be.

"Lemme fix it." I wiped away the streaks gently, and she hated me less. "You should put some on for real though."

"Ma will be mad," she said.

"Nah, she won't be," I said.

"I don't know how."

"Me neither," I said.

She sat mostly still while I applied it. Her top lip British Red and the bottom Nude. Clio gave me Divine Wine. We pursed our lips in the mirror and posed, over and over again, each one more dramatic than the last. We thought we looked like Naomi Campbell, when she was twelve and eleven at least. We pressed our fingers into Mrs. Vanessa's eyeshadows and left fingerprints in the mauve and matte blues. We poked each other in the eye more than we actually applied anything, but our eyelids were peacocks. We revealed our flashy colors to each other. We covered ourselves in glitter body spray and couldn't stop smelling the parts on our wrists where the perfume clung the most.

We returned the bathroom to its former virgin state. The drawers and medicine cabinet closed, leaving no trace of the deflowering we'd done. Ma and Lonnie were still pairs of legs on the couch, Ma's painted toes caressing his hairy hobbit ones.

Lonnie and Mrs. Vanessa's bed was always made just right. I thought they must have never slept in it. Some of Vanessa's dresses, still on their hangers, were laid out on the bed. They must have been the ones she chose not to take. Lonnie was probably supposed to hang them back up, but he hadn't. We hoped for his sake that when she came back on Tuesday, he would have. We crinkled the blanket and creased her clothes with our bodies, rolling around on top of them.

The dresses slipped on easily over our heads, though they hung too long and too loose. So suddenly, we were women. Clio's dress had silver buttons all the way down the front. She shoved her hands into the two front pockets and admired herself from every angle in the floor-length mirror. Mine was yellow, with a hole in the back where my birthmark was visible. I remembered how Ma said that God made yellow just for Black girls. We couldn't walk in Vanessa's shoes, they were too high, but we could stand for a few seconds before our ankles wobbled enough that we fell back against the bed, laughing.

"What's going on in here?" Lonnie asked.

We froze, sure there was only trouble to come and thinking of the best way to get out of it. Clio, certain that as long as Ma didn't see, there was no evidence, began undoing the buttons.

"No, no, no. Don't worry," Lonnie said. He helped her button them back up. Her hands hung in the air, the barely visible hairs standing straight up. His knees popped as he leaned down, his face a few inches from mine. Some of my curly baby hairs about to brush against the coarse unshaved shadow of a beard, the Pretty Lady tickling my cheeks when he spoke.

"You little ladies having fun?" he asked.

"We'll take it off," Clio said.

He brought his thumb up to his mouth and sucked on it for a moment. He slowly swiped the curve of my bottom lip with his wet finger.

"This stuff's tricky. You'll get the hang of it. You want me to teach you a trick? Gimme your hand."

My limbs stayed stuck to my sides, tingling to the edge of pain, going numb until I couldn't remember whether it was a symptom of a heart attack or a stroke. Ma had tried to make us memorize what signals our bodies would send under life-threatening causes so that we could save each other, but right then, when it mattered, I couldn't tell you what was wrong.

"No?" he asked.

Lonnie gently pressed his finger against my lips, probing for resistance. "Just open."

I don't know what magic prompted my mouth to pop open. He put his thumb in my mouth, and my lips closed around it.

Ma says the best way to get a man's attention is to put something in your mouth. She and my Aunt Tonya had been walking back home after the concert; they were young, sixteen or seventeen. A limo pulled up, the window rolled down, and a Black hand with a Rolex around the wrist beckoned them both closer.

Ma leaned into the car, breasts first. They were still perky then, not yet ravaged by Clio and I. Michael, the bass, was her favorite. She was glad he was the one doing the talking. His voice slid over her like silk pajamas and soft red-carpet gowns. He promised champagne and a late night, but all my mother heard was a baby if she played her cards right. No more sockets that spit fire when you tried to plug something in, no more falling onto the floor while the men outside shot the building full of holes, no more hoping that the old woman next door wasn't the one to catch a bullet in the neck, no more splitting a one-bedroom apartment with four sisters and two cousins.

Once, she had sent us to bed while Aunt Tonya was over and they laughed about how stupid they were then. Me and Clio lay on the floor, heads rubbing together while we peeked through the slip of light at the bottom of the door. They were dancing, with hips a little wider and less flexible than they used to be, but me and Clio could imagine them then, curly hair in '90s asymmetrical cuts, small dresses, borrowed shoes, and Bath and Body Works Japanese Cherry Blossom perfume. Tonya said they should've done it all differently. She would've never met LeRoy and wouldn't work at the chicken factory now if she had just let one of them take her. Ma said she would take her life as it is because sleeping in that other room would probably be a Michelle and a Holly. And who the fuck would they be? Not those girls. Those weird, smart, fucked-up girls. I had never known that Ma liked us. Loved us, of course, but not liked.

"Besides," Ma laughed, "who's to say even if we did, they wouldn't have just dropped us off at the nearest Scrape 'N' Save and kept on moving?"

They both knew she was right, but a ho life past is still a life mourned.

"Purse your lips," Lonnie said.

"What?" my voice muffled.

"Purse your lips."

I couldn't. So he used his other hand to squish my face, and he pulled out his finger with a definitive pop. A ring of purple around his thumb.

"This way it stays off your teeth," he said.

I nodded.

"Valentina's in the backyard. She's got your present back there."

It was a trampoline. Ma was smiling in the backyard with a beer in her hand while she clapped her hands and said things like "This is so nice of him!" and "Tell him thank you. He didn't have to do this." When we didn't fall all over ourselves in thanking him, Ma looked at the two of us hard.

The least you can do is act grateful, Ma thought.

So we were grateful. For hours we were grateful. Clio pushed through the mesh net and pulled me through. I crawled my way across the smooth landscape until Clio jumped and I fell face down. The canvas was hot and burned my face.

I saw Ma sitting on Lonnie's lap; they leaned back in a lounge chair as she kissed his neck. His eyes were on us. We bounced together and didn't stop when they laughed, or kissed, or when they disappeared inside, and we bounced to feel like we weren't alone. The blinds were partly open, so we bounced to feel like they were closed, and we bounced to feel like we couldn't see inside. We bounced as the sun went down, and we bounced when they asked if we wanted to order pizza. We bounced until the food came, we took our portions and lay on our backs, breathing heavy from our tiredness. We bounced and promised each other when the rapture happened the last thing we put our eyes on would be each other. We bounced until the neighborhood went quiet, and the moon hung, we bounced while we held hands, we bounced while Clio wiped a stray tear from my cheek, we bounced and watched the whole families in their own private spaces, we bounced while I asked Clio if she thought our father ever really loved us, we bounced until Ma told us it was time to go home.

I let Clio ride shotgun. The stop sign that said *Get Fucked* was gone. A new one was already in place. I remember rolling the backseat window down and wondering if I was gonna forget someday, about him, lipstick, trampolines. I did. For a while. And then, it came back. Three days ago, on my fifteenth birthday, I kissed a boy, Cameron. When his tongue slipped past my lips, I found it there behind my teeth. I was surprised he didn't pull away, that he couldn't feel it.

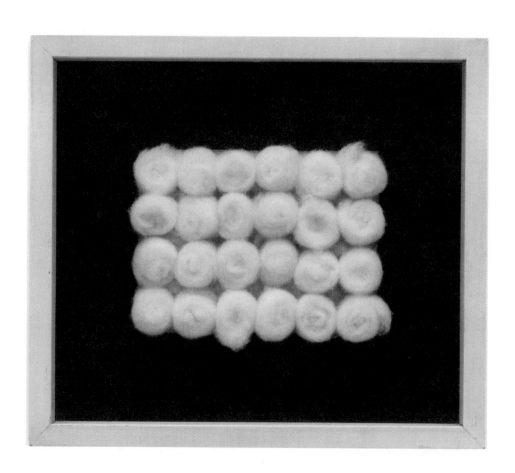

Piero Manzoni, *Achrome*. 1961-1962.

FICTION / KATE DOYLE

WE'LL BE ALONE

Her professor is sorry Meg hates it here, but Meg says, *Oh, it's fine.* It is, in the sense that she's handling it: She's come to ask for a recommendation to transfer. When her letter came last April, her parents poured champagne, and Meg felt accomplished, pleased, only passingly hesitant. Now, most days, after her one P.M. English class, she gets into bed and does not wake up until after the room is steeped in darkness.

———

When her father called last night, the ring of the phone pulled her up from a dream of vast oceany sadness, whose details slipped from her like water. She tried to make her voice sound alert as she answered. At one point in their conversation, he said to her, gently, *You just have to just calm your emotions, and you will be fine there.* Meg stayed quiet. She did not say, *Please don't tell me how I'll be.*

———

In high school she was studious, she was responsible, she was fine, and now it's like something warm and animating is drained from her. In the fall she took long showers to avoid her roommate, cheerful Laura Heller, obviously thriving: always off to intramural tennis, to a cappella, to play rehearsal. Meg slept whole afternoons, sliding through blurry dreams. She filled out paperwork to move to a single room. In December her parents picked her up, and with the dean's approval she wrote final papers from the family room. *She's recuperating*, she heard her mother say to someone on the phone, as if this were a cold. *How are you*, said her father, and she pretended not to hear, raised the volume on the television.

———

It's February now, a new semester. Her professor's windows frame an expanse of vacant, snowy quad. Sometimes the weather is all Meg can say to articulate any of this: *It's so cold here*, she'll say. Last week her mother mailed her a new, warmer coat. Today Meg unsealed it from the box, laid it out across the bed.

———

Now she zips the coat up to her chin as her professor promises a copy of her letter by email next week. *I hope you find the thing you're looking for*, he says as she is standing up to leave. Meg makes a grateful, noncommittal sound, aware she radiates embarrassment as she goes. Moments later, in the hall, trying to dig her phone out of her bag, she walks into someone getting off the elevator.

———

The girl wears a blue wool coat; she has unruly, pretty hair. *Sorry*, she says, though it wasn't precisely her fault, and they revolve around each other in a performance of improved carefulness—Meg laughing forcefully, too brightly. The other girl grasps her arm as if to navigate, then lets go. When Meg looks up, she expects to see her retreating down the hall, but instead she's still there, paused, half-smiling, the clarity of her interest unsettling. The closing door slips between them, but even so Meg steps back—an impulse that feels close to self-defense. Any time she reflects on it later (minutes, years) she won't be able to decide: Was this good instinct, a kind of intuition? Or just regular, unsubstantiated, stupid fear?

———

A much later girlfriend, the one Meg nearly marries, will say the moment sort of torments her. *Let's keep it need to know with exes*, Sara will say, laughing in a way that's maybe supposed to sound causal. *I don't like knowing how you and Jenny met.* Meg and Sara have been together only a month at this point, but Sara's dread of anything intruding, even a memory, will feel familiar; it will remind Meg of the year she applied to transfer, and of Jenny, and her pulse will quicken. *You should tell me about meeting me instead, how great that was*, Sara is saying in that same half-joking tone, reaching to refill their wineglasses. Meg is looking out the window behind Sara, where the light in the dusk sky is beginning to turn. *What are you looking at?* says Sara, and she smiles, looks over her shoulder.

———

With Sara it was a birthday party in Fort Greene, the summer Meg moved to Brooklyn from uptown. Sara in a pink dress, leaning on the bar. *Wait, you two don't know each other?* says the host, putting her hand to her forehead, like this is an unfathomable oversight. And Sara says—eyebrows raised—*We don't*. With Jenny it was the elevator in the English Department, the winter of freshman year. And as Sara sets the wine bottle back on the table, Meg will seem to hear Jenny, tempting Meg for her attention: *You should tell me about meeting me instead, how great that was.*

———

By the time the letter of recommendation to transfer appears in her inbox, Meg will have seen the elevator girl three times. First there in the English Department: the *sorry*, their physical proximity, the door like a film transition as it slid across the girl's face. The next time forty minutes later down in the foyer, where Meg could not afterward explain precisely why she sat down and stayed there, reading, until the point when this girl reemerged: crossing the empty foyer, talking on her cell phone, not noticing Meg. Opening one of the front doors, closing it, gone.

———

(*I did see you actually*, Jenny will admit, some weeks later. She'll say, *I was being cool. I had smiled like such a weirdo upstairs, then I did it again when I saw you there, so—I just put my head down and got out. It was my sister on the phone. She said, "What's happening, you sound weird."*)

———

Everywhere on campus, all week, Meg looks. It isn't the elevator girl buying coffee in the student center, nor her swiping into a West Campus dorm—though Meg detours in both cases to be certain. Then, over the weekend, her old roommate

Laura Heller throws a party. The text reads: *Maybe you would want to come?* Meg's mother is always saying, *Maybe you'd feel better if you spent more time with people*; all evidence to the contrary, Meg retains the hope it could be true. Wearing the new coat, she is marginally warmer than she's been in weeks, making her way to the party under falling tufts of snow, crossing the total silence of the long, empty quad. Up the steps, inside, the party is dim, full of chatter, with a warm-body smell like the beach at low tide. She almost turns and leaves. Instead she pours a drink and looks around for anyone she knows here, in this room with its low sloping ceilings, its old windows thickly paned, its familiar but differently arranged decorations—this room that Laura Heller moved to after Meg moved out.

––––––

Improbably, Meg's eyes light on the elevator girl, surfacing from the shadowy far side of the room. She wears a short skirt, green sweater, and severe, lovely eye shadow (which in time, Jenny will dispute—*I would not ever*, she'll say, her laughter alarmed, incredulous, *I'd look ridiculous*, but Meg will say, *No, no, you looked good, I loved it*). Meg takes a long, steadying sip, and her legs feel strange and soft. She is a new drinker this semester, has only very recently abandoned her resolve never, ever to be someone who drinks, and so the alcohol gets to her fast, and the memory of what's said here will always be blurry. (Jenny will always insist it was Meg who spoke first, who said—but this always seems so unlikely—*Hello, it's you.* Whereas Meg remembers saying a half sentence, then deciding not to finish it. Feeling herself flush and warm. Wanting to be close to and far from the elevator girl.)

––––––

In the year they stay together, Jenny will always be riffing on it. *Hello, it's you*, she'll say when she lets Meg into her room, or she'll pick up the phone saying, *Meg, it's you!* Meg says, *Jenny, that doesn't sound like me at all.* Mostly it's a joke, a flirtation tense with affection, with controversy. Something to laugh about, spar about, something to stake claims on: their origin story. Then one night it won't be funny—*I know what I heard*, Jenny will say, reaching to close the door as they leave Meg's room, and Meg's enjoyment will dissolve. *You must not even know me*, she'll say in the ensuing argument—crying indulgently, sitting in the dorm stairwell. Confusingly bereft, her head in her hands, rain pounding on the skylight several stories up. Jenny will sit beside her and move her hand in gentle circles on Meg's back. *What the fuck*, she'll say. *Of course I do.*

———

But Meg remembers this part clearly: Jenny explaining she's in a play with Laura Heller. Meg says, *How is the play?* and Jenny says, *Oh God, so bad, but it's too late to quit. They'd be stuck if I left now. Believe me, I've considered it.* They take a pair of shots. They sit together on the sill of Laura Heller's window, which has a cold draft sifting under it. Meg can recall condemning, not discreetly, Laura's taste in general—*I hated that poster, when we were roommates*, she says over the music, into this girl's ear, pointing.

———

They kiss—Jenny, who hasn't even yet told Meg her name, making the move to push one hand up the side of Meg's neck and jaw and into her hair. Meg leans back against the window so the girl can move in closer, and the cold glass through her shirt is excruciating on her shoulder blades, the knots of her spine.

———

Her hands in this girl's lovely hair. The girl's hand moving down Meg's forearm, then her waist and her leg, as they kiss for the length of a song, then another, then part of a third until the girl pulls back, and says—trying not to smile, maybe, her shirt sort of askew and so close Meg admires the dark eye shadow—*Want to go to my room? I live upstairs.*

———

She holds out her hand, a joke, as if to shake hello. *I'm Jenny.* Then she raises her eyebrows: So? And actually, Meg does want to go—but also she wants to stay where they are. Significance floods her, and briefly, with satisfaction, she imagines the cold from outside enveloping the room, their breath in clouds, ice forming in Jenny's hair, a preservation.

––––––––

Lately any time Meg calls home and says, *Everything is different, I can't take it*, her father tells her, *Life is change*. Her mother says, *You'll be all right*. Now Meg is shivering, agitated by this sense she has so often lately that something essential is leaching out of her, everything the loss of something else. *Come here*, she wants to tell this girl. *Stay here*. Instead she nods more or less normally: Yes. And she takes the girl's hand for the joke, small and warm.

––––––––

While the elevator girl—Jenny—hunts for her purse on the shadowy far side of the room, Meg hovers by the door, shifts her weight from one foot to the other. Jenny is telling a handful of friends that she's leaving. She pushes her unruly hair behind her ear, adjusts a barrette, looks pointedly over her shoulder. So now all the friends' eyes move to Meg, by the door. She tries to shift her own gaze casually to her phone. Tries not to signal Laura Heller is the only person she knows here, opts to suppress the question of whether she is doing something stupid. A text from her father resolves on the screen: *Good night*.

––––––––

Out in the hall then. Their paired, padding footsteps on dimly lit stairs. *Sorry for my dumb friends back there*, Jenny's saying. They kiss more on the landing, Jenny's hand just touching Meg at the side of her face, the cinder block wall on Meg's back, then Jenny's, and now Jenny is fixing her hair again, unlocking her door, making a small performance of this, like they're in some old movie: *Won't you come in?*

––––––––

The door swings open; it's dark inside. Jenny shakes her hand free from the sleeve of her coat, reaches her fingers to flip the light switch. (But actually that's Meg's coat she's wearing, which seems premature, and what's more they never went outside on this night, only upstairs to the fifth floor. So this part is misordered, transplanted? This part is another time. On another night entirely, Jenny is saying, in that same old-Hollywood voice, *Get in here, would you?* Taking Meg by the wrist, drawing her closer.)

———

But this part Meg remembers, this is clear: a tentative snow in the half-lit dark outside the window. She remembers lifting Jenny's shirt over her head, Jenny saying something and laughing. Jenny's snaky ribs, this nervous closeness. Later, the streetlight seeping in through fogged glass over Jenny's small form. Her tangled long hair, taking over the pillow like a weed.

———

Meg likes, as they fade into sleeping, the intimacy of all this hair—so close to her face it's practically up her nose. Likes the square of light on Jenny's cheekbone from outside, and her sleep-muttering, the sharp certain tossing of her head thrown back on the pillow. The seethe and clank of the dorm radiator, and the footsteps and low voices, brief laughing and shushing of roommates in the common area. The line of gold light under the door, and then how it goes away.

———

In the dark, both of them breathing. All night as they turn in their sleep, knocking around together like two small boats. This bed will never be enough room for them, it will always be uncomfortable, but Meg loves it entirely, possessed by a nostalgia that infects her straightaway. Cold through the drafty window. Pink-patterned sheets. One pillow shared between them, until they go and buy a second one some weeks later—which, even this early, Meg will feel is sort of poisoning the way things had once been. Jenny tossing and turning: this thing she has about which sides of herself she can and cannot sleep on, and why, why not. Meg's thing about hating to sleep by the wall, her insistence on the possibility of extrication. She has a memory of Jenny in her worn out high school track shirt, sometime later this semester, out of bed with a towel on her arm saying, *We could literally move my bed, if you hate your side so much*. Meg says sleepily into the new pillow, *But I don't want to move your bed*.

————

In New York, five years later, Sara's bed will be objectively better. Warmer, more spacious, of course. Meg will sometimes joke, *Remember college? Remember twin beds?* And Sara will laugh and say, *I really try to forget*. The first summer they're together, in Brooklyn, the year that both of them are twenty-five, they forge a kind of ritual from the awful heat of Sara's room: drinking cold wine with a whirring box fan pointed toward them, stretched out on this bed with its nest of too many pillows. *No, don't throw them away*, Meg will say, when Sara tries to prune a few, *I like them all*, and Sara will laugh and say, *You never want anything to go*. Most nights Sara's dog will sleep between them. They wake up in the night and laugh and feel irritated and push the dog's sleeping weight around the bed. On several bleary mornings, they make a joke of shaking their fists at the dog together: *Stop being difficult, you jerk. Stay still, stay*.

————

Here is where they take each other's clothes off. Here is where they lie checking email on their phones, feet touching. Here is where they go to sleep seething, any time they fight. Here is where they face each other one late-summer night, Sara's roommates' video games blaring sounds of carnage and loss and *game over* just past the closed bedroom door, a warm wind moving swiftly in the window. The dog resettles his chin on Meg's bare ankle, as Sara fixes a loose piece of Meg's hair with her fingers and says, half-kidding: *You and I would have three kids, obviously. Two would be predictable and honestly dull*. Meg laughs and moves her hand along Sara's wrist. She feels, exquisitely, hope.

————

The rush of air from the box fan reminds her of the drafty window in Jenny's room. This summer when she first meets Sara, Meg looks up Jenny Evert on the internet—a habit she thought she'd broken but which seems, again, to beckon, to wrap its hand around her wrist. *Come here*. Jenny Evert has moved to Austin, Texas; she does marketing for a community arts nonprofit. It could be that she's dating the woman in this photo, whose arm is around Jenny's waist. To look at this picture makes Meg feel vaguely ill, time overtaking her in a nauseous wave. Then she imagines what if Sara walked in now, and the itchiness of guilt overtakes her. *Please stop talking about all these stupid things*, she remembers Jenny telling her on the phone once—just after Meg transferred to Columbia, when they were taking the bus back and forth on weekends. In the memory Jenny says, *I worry about you, like you'll never enjoy your actual life. You never let anything go.* Even now Meg can still replay each word, subtly accusatory, quietly furious, like a curse being placed: *You never stop dwelling on all your old stuff.*

———

And this is going to sound bad, but whatever—I don't want to not enjoy my life, because of the way that you are. I don't want you dragging me down.

———

From the beginning, they fight—it's embarrassing, shocking. They argue in public, or else alone in one of their rooms: draining, circular conversations, discordant and cruel, slipping beyond their control. *Don't be so stupid*, Jenny will tell her sometimes, pacing like a provoked animal. All her life Meg will be ashamed to remember the mutual, ready animosity—beginning so early, even the first morning after the first night, both of them sleepy, warm, Jenny reaching her hand to untwist the sheet where it's caught around Meg's shoulder and saying with a kind of hesitation in her voice, *I've sort of been imagining running into you all week.* And then something unclasps, and Meg finds she can't contain this panic, billowing. *I don't want you to imagine me*, she says, *I'm a real person, I have a whole life. You only just met me.* Jenny takes her hand back. Her hair is messy around her face; she looks injured. *Of course*, she says, *I know*—but Meg is seized by a fretful compulsion to say well this was nice but she's going to leave. She starts to sit up but can't quite free herself from the sheets. Jenny says, *Hey, I was being romantic.* Meg says, wresting her own foot from a tangle of blankets, *Look maybe you won't understand this, but I don't want you to act some special way. Let's not be people who pretend.*

―――――

I'm going to go shower, says Jenny. *I don't really know what we're talking about.*

―――――

Sun through the window over the place where Jenny slept. Meg reaches for her coat draped over the desk chair, for her phone in the pocket (*warning, low battery*), where she finds in her inbox an email from her professor with, see attached, her letter. She waits for the sound of the tap coming on in the bathroom before she opens the attachment, in which she is praised especially for her passionate responses to assigned readings. This is a commendation so mysteriously saddening that she turns off her phone without reading anything more. By the time Jenny comes back, Meg has both her hands over her face. *Hey*, says Jenny then, softening—wrapped in a towel, her hair wet. She sits down on the edge of the bed, puts her arm around Meg's shoulder.

―――――

That night Meg is in the library, methodically entering full name, date of birth, address into application forms, when Jenny texts. *Come over? Or I'll come to you?* Meg logs out. She calls home while she walks, because she was supposed to call this weekend. Tonight the calm certainty in her father's voice bothers her strangely as she picks her way over the snowbanks of the hushed campus moonscape. *Anyway, I should get back to these applications*, she says, and waves her ID to test if it can swipe her into Jenny's building.

―――――

Help, no card access! You have to come get me.

Hello it's you! I'm coming.

―――――

Good night, says her dad. *Take care.* Waiting for Jenny to open the door, Meg thinks of what her mother said, all but sternly, just a few weeks earlier: *If you're this unhappy, I think something has to change.* The two of them in her mother's closet, familiar smelling, with its wool sweaters, its folded pants, its green ceramic dish of loose change and jewelry. Looking for extra, warmer socks Meg can take back with her, because of the cold. Her mother reaches a hand to search around a high shelf. *There's no reason to stay anywhere that feels this bad to you*, she's saying. Meg looks down at her own feet on the floor of her mother's closet and feels a familiar sensation of illogical hope that sometimes comes to her, fluttering up through dread—a passing belief in the potential for some shift or transformation. She runs her finger along the lip of the ceramic bowl. She says: *When do you know for sure it's too late for things to get better? When do you know that you just have to move on?*

————

The night she and Jenny have their most truly brutal fight, she'll remember that question, after hours of argument at Meg's apartment near Columbia—her roommate at the library, the two of them liberated to storm around, to cry, to call each other names. Eventually they're quiet, exhausted, finally stalled, Jenny silent and still on the edge of the bed, Meg lying on the floor looking up at the ceiling. *How can you know if something is fundamentally bad*, she says finally, *versus only currently? How do you know if something is temporary, or if it's the way it will always be?* Jenny will deflate back into the heap of Meg's unmade bed. She'll seem to think about that, seem to linger on the brink of some response—but she will not, in the end, say anything, and the two of them will lie in silence as the evening deepens into blue, and all the traffic in the street keeps up its clamor.

————

Agitated, through the hours of this argument, Meg has pulled and pulled and pulled at a loose thread in her sleeve, so much it gets unraveled around her wrist. Eventually Jenny gets up from the bed and says she's going to take a walk, she wants to be alone, and she's closing the door behind her before Meg realizes in a wave of pure, giddy, furious irritation: She'll certainly have to throw this sweater away. It would be gratifying, she considers, to burn the sweater on the fire escape. To shred it with scissors. To consign it fatally to the kitchen trash. Instead, alone with the quiet clicking of her radiator, she sits up and lifts the sweater over her head. Carefully, she folds it into a plastic bag, so she won't forget to take it somewhere to be donated or recycled or whatever. But then it's like fuck it, and she takes the scissors and does cut up the whole, soft pouch—surgically, over the trash, an experiment in destructiveness that leaves her crying so much her face aches, crying so much she imagines what if Jenny could hear her from the street. Afterward, she falls asleep on her bed, its mass of sheets, one lamp still on. Jenny comes back later, asks her, *Do you want a shirt?* But Meg pretends that she's still sleeping, twists her face away. Jenny lies down, turns off the light, and puts her hand on Meg's back.

———

It's when Meg is following Jenny to her dorm room the second time ever, in the weird glowy light of the dorm stairwell, that it occurs to her to say something about transferring. Not yet though, she decides—pleasurably woozy, back in this girl's company. Smoothing her fingers along the blue metal banister, feeling her face warm in the new heat of indoors. It would be premature.

———

But then they spend the next—was it five nights? Five—together. Three at Jenny's, one at hers, Jenny's again. *We could make a bad habit of this*, Meg is saying, unwinding her scarf, as Jenny lets her in the third or fourth time. *Or else the best habit ever*, Jenny is saying, and kissing her, as Meg is slipping her hands, still trailing the scarf, around the back of Jenny's neck.

———

The sixth night she lies she has an assignment: *I really shouldn't. I have to write this paper.* At her desk as she drafts the personal essay for her applications, she can see the snow that crowns the hill outside her window turn gold, then lavender, then bleak gray, until the rural darkness blots it out—all but one eerie swathe of glow from the nearest campus blue-light box. *I am looking for opportunities to feel better.* Backspace, *be warmer.* Backspace, be serious, *pursue my education in an urban setting.* She closes her phone in her desk while she works. It rings once, a muted trill: her father, the voicemail says, when she checks eventually. Just saying hi and he'll try again tomorrow. And here is a text from Jenny, waiting: *I want to play this cooler than I am, but I wish you were here.*

———

Somewhere, in the sinuous walkways of the dark campus, happy laughter rings. The text scares her; she doesn't know why. Curled on her side on the bed, she deletes it.

———

The next day, in the dining hall, she doesn't answer her mother's call. Not the day after that, either, walking back from French, though the phone rings literally in her hand as she's texting *Tonight?*—her gloves precarious where she's wedged them between her arm and ribs so she can type. To her mother, she writes, *Can't talk but I'm fine, I'll call soon.* In the morning her father calls, but she's in Jenny's kitchen and doesn't answer that, either: Jenny barefoot in running shorts and her old cross country sweatshirt, cold light from the window illumining her jaw and hair, measuring out coffee grounds with a spoon. *I can't wait for this coffee,* she's saying. A roommate emerges, wincing, and greets Jenny in a low voice, before she notices Meg and adds, with an effortful summoning of interest, *Hi.* Meg starts to respond, but with a movement of her hand the roommate insinuates she's hungover and doesn't wish to converse. She carries herself to the shower, snaps the bathroom door shut behind her so curtly that Jenny brandishes the spoon after Dana—or was it Ellen? Well, one of them. In a low voice, she says, *Rude. Next year: a single room. Think of it. We'll be alone.*

———

She says it again: *Alone.* Does this suggestive, amazing thing with her eyebrows that makes Meg burst out laughing, and decide not to mention she has no plans to be here next year.

———

Jenny will always be making this sort of remark: *next year* and *after we graduate* and *someday*. One night, walking together to Meg's room, Jenny behind her as they move along an icy bit of narrow sidewalk, snow encroaching from each side, Jenny says, *Sometime we should live together, and then it won't always be like, do I even have clothes I can wear tomorrow?* Meg laughs softly: *You can wear my clothes.* Jenny says, *That would be sort of cute. Okay, I like that idea.*

———

Sara says, *Hang on*, and looks up from the fridge. She says, *Seriously?* Because it makes no sense, Meg and Jenny, barely knowing each other a month and talking like that. Meg says, setting the last dish to dry in the rack, wringing out a sponge to wipe down Sara's counter: *I know—sometimes I feel like I must be remembering things out of order. But I think we were just super young? Things move fast and you're an idiot.*

———

Sara says, *No, I mean like are you actually telling me this? I mean what was this—six years ago?* Meg says, *Oh*, and it feels like there's some explanation to make, but her mouth can't find it. *Let me do that*, says Sara, and it's vicious somehow, the way she takes the sponge. The drag of her short fingernails over Meg's wet palms.

———

In the play, Jenny is wonderful. On a little folding chair, in the dark black box theater, Meg is thrilled, small shivers course her spine, she wraps her arms around herself. She feels gripped with possibility, she regrets having come here with Dana and Ellen and Ellen's boyfriend—the three of them in chairs to her left, their intermittent and distracting whispers. She wishes she'd come tomorrow, had come alone. She misses an essential plot point of one scene, just imagining this other way it could have been. She twists her hands together in her lap. Distracted, afterward, she forgets her gloves under her chair.

———

And she hates having to greet Jenny in the company of others, having to share her. She can't speak: Jenny, striking in her stage makeup, is buoyant, is joyful, is embracing her friends, some of whom Meg recognizes. She's wearing the green wool cardigan, hair gathered up at the back of her neck, and someone's given her a bunch of daisies in green tissue and clear plastic, which she has in her arms as if holding a baby. Laura Heller materializes. Meg tries to summon something of her performance—*You were so good*, she tries, and Laura's thanks are effusive. She points at Jenny's lipstick on Meg's cheek: *You guys are cute.*

———

Years from now, Meg will run into Laura Heller at a party in Brooklyn. They will be happy to see one another, will entirely enjoy catching up. Eventually Laura will say, as she opens another beer for each of them, *I always felt responsible for you and Jenny Evert meeting*, and she will look faintly proud of herself, and Meg will be surprised by the savageness of her own reply, and the way it makes Laura's face go blank, humiliated: *You absolutely weren't.*

———

After the play there is a basically torturous group dinner that Laura has organized, at the BYOB sushi place off campus. *We don't have to go*, says Jenny, putting on her coat, though plainly she intends to. At the restaurant everyone seems to be friends with everyone: roommates, castmates, roommates of castmates, everyone Jenny knows, it feels like, talking over one other, passing huge cheap bottles of wine down the table.

———

So it isn't until afterward that Meg gets Jenny alone long enough to say anything. And this was the I love you: on College Avenue, outside the sushi place. Cars easing by, their lights catching the shimmer of heaped curbside snowbanks. Still in the crook of Jenny's arm, these daises in paper and cellophane, the plastic crinkled between Jenny and Meg's two coats. Meg's bare hands in Jenny's hair, and Jenny, joking: *So not, ultimately, such a terrible night for you?*

———

Later, Jenny's falling-asleep breath is even along Meg's collarbone; she seems asleep, but then *I love you* she says again, and moves her hair out of her face, settles herself closer, touches her forehead to Meg's shoulder. Meg stares fixedly into the shadowed form of the daisies bunched together in their cup—visible over Jenny's head, as if an outgrowth of the hair.

———

A slant of streetlight through the window falls over Jenny's nose and the daisies in their drinking glass and makes, through the water, a murky amoeba of faint light on the surface of the desk. Meg has an impulse to ask who the flowers are from, but doesn't. Long after Jenny really does fall asleep, Meg wonders in the dark, considers in turn every person she saw tonight. Certain possibilities upset her. *Jenny?* she says quietly, but Jenny doesn't stir.

———

Meg moves her face away from Jenny's hair so she can breathe. Wants a glass of water but can't get up, because she's next to the stupid wall. *The thing is,* Jenny says to her in the dining hall the next morning, or maybe the one after— some morning this week, anyway, plunging her fork into the soft yolk of her poached egg—*I don't know why you have to ask me that way. So suspicious. Like I could ask you why you didn't bring me flowers. But I didn't ask you that, you know?*

———

Then someone they know passes by their table, and Jenny brightens to hide what's going on. Waves.

———

Meg is home for a weekend. Her father is making pasta, her mother setting the table, when Meg asks, *When are you supposed to ignore what you're afraid of, and when are you supposed to pay attention?* In general, she's been wondering, Is it better to ask a question if you're afraid you know the answer—better to get what you fear out in the open? Or should you leave it alone and hope the thought will go away—hope it won't persist, becoming more complex, obsessive, tangled, confused? *What exactly is it that's concerning you?* her dad asks, and he starts adding capers to the sauce, angling the small glass jar. Meg's sitting on the counter and wants to explain her state of mind, but can't exactly. She kicks her heels against the loose door of the lower cabinet. *Careful*, says her mother.

————

At some point she realizes she shouldn't wait any longer to tell them. Outside the library, pacing the gridded, neat courtyard, tucking her face down into her scarf, she calls home. It's snowing again, of course—the afternoon daylight flat and strange through low clouds. *How nice*, says her mother. *You sound better. Will we meet her when we pick you up at spring break? Why don't we all go to lunch?* Below, down the hill to the quad, Meg can see the knitting and unknitting lines of other students: crawling here and there, to class, from class, library, dining hall, gym. After she hangs up, on her way to Jenny's room, taking the stairs down the long hill—cradling her bag close, because this wet snow is coming down hard now—she already misses the time before she told them anything. When Jenny was only hers.

————

This is a confusing sensation that makes her feel so stupid. She shakes her head, as if it might be possible to the disperse the feeling, but it seems only to squeeze her more tightly. And here is Jenny walking toward her: head bent. Her hair starred with caught bits of snow. They're inside before Jenny notices anything: *Oh no*, she says finally, *What is it, what's wrong?* On the vestibule floor, slush from their boots is already resolving into melty puddles, some of the snow in Jenny's hair changed to shiny dabs of water. Meg says, *I don't know, I don't know.* She frees one of her hands from its glove and holds on for one moment to Jenny's hand, then reaches up to wipe her own eyes with her fist, so tears smear along the skin of her hand.

————

Upstairs, in Jenny's room, they hang their coats, scarves, gloves to dry on the desk chair, on the radiator, by spare hangers from dresser drawers. They put their boots together to dry on a towel. In the bed, they lie close: Jenny on her back, hair damp, reading this long book she has to finish for a seminar tomorrow. She has her book in one hand and the other arm around Meg, who's curled on her side, French workbook open on the quilt to her assigned conjugations. She takes her pen and draws little swirls and jags, pulses in the margin. The radiator clucks, then sighs. Meg says, finally, *Do your parents know about me?* And she can feel Jenny shift then, her breath on Meg's hair and the back of her neck. *Um yes*, says Jenny, and Meg can feel her smile. Later that night, in the common room kitchen, Meg will tell her about transferring. Jenny will clench a hand around her glass so hard the water she's drinking will shiver in its cup, and Meg will stand instinctively. *Stop*, she'll say, *Just wait*, but Jenny is already talking, voice ragged, rising, insistent, changed, like someone else, like not Jenny at all, she says, *So many people want to go to school here. Do you know that people want to go to school here?* She says, *Honestly. What is actually wrong with you?*

———

Sara will ask Meg to meet her parents when they have only been dating a few weeks. The two of them drinking Bloody Marys on an overcast Sunday, some brunch place in Crown Heights. Meg will say something about remembering to call her parents, and Sara will swirl her ice with her celery and say, hey speaking of parents, why doesn't Meg come out to New Jersey next weekend?

———

Jesus, Meg will say, unexpectedly saddened. As if something is ending too soon. Later, she'll be unable to decide if Sara's behavior in this instance shows her to have solid instincts or betrays a fundamental recklessness. *What if we hadn't worked out*, Meg will ask through a mouthful of toothpaste, however many months later. Brushing her teeth, wearing a borrowed sweater of Sara's, coming to stand in the doorway to her room. *We might still not work out*, says Sara, sitting on the bed, stroking the dog's forehead so its eyes wink closed. *I just thought it would make you happy to be asked.* Behind her in the window, the afternoon light is bright and clear, and Meg knows what Sara wants to hear: *Of course we'll work out.* Actually, she wants to hear it too. But before either of them can say anything, Sara's roommate comes home. *Hey hey*, he says pleasantly, and as he hangs up his bike helmet on the hook by the door, it seems easier to say nothing. Meg looks away from Sara, out the window again.

————

When Ellen comes home, Meg is disappointed. She and Jenny have been curled around each other on the couch. Earlier they started a movie but, *You're missing the whole thing* said Jenny when she noticed Meg looking out the window, looking at the snow as it fell. Half-amused, Jenny paused the television, and now they're just talking, watching the snow. Then Ellen is interrupting in the doorway, stomping slush from her boots, stripping away wet layers, going on about how oh, she loves this movie. What were they watching, even? Usually Meg can summon up old details, but in this case she doesn't have it. Nothing but an onscreen image, paused: some landscape, rugged. Impossible to place.

————

We have homework, Jenny lies to Ellen, before they retreat to Jenny's room, close the door, fall on the bed laughing and shushing each other—which is why, in joking despair, Jenny says, *But homework!* as Meg is reaching for her. *Maybe for you*, says Meg, kissing Jenny's face, her neck, moving the edge of her shirt to reach her collarbone: *I'm on my way out. No consequences.*

————

She means it as a joke, but Jenny presses her forehead to Meg's shoulder and stays there, very still. Months later, she'll look at the acceptance letters lined up on Meg's desk with feral anger—like she could kill them with her teeth, the perfect envelopes.

————

They try staying together. Her parents say, *For a place you really hated, you're still spending so much time there.* When she and Jenny break up, Meg figures it will be a sort of trial thing. An experiment of some protracted agony, involving regular check-in phone calls. Later an agreement to stop texting, so they can give each other space. Then maybe Jenny taking the bus down to Columbia, where they will find that time apart has eased their problems. Just imagining it floods Meg with warmth. But this, actually, will be the last time they ever see each other: Jenny, not crying, hails a taxi on Amsterdam. Her right hand raised in the air, one early morning.

———

Sara's parents live near the beach. On the bright fall day Meg goes to meet them, the dog comes too. Meg walks with Sara and her parents by the water and lets the dog off leash—they watch it run the scalloping shoreline, muscles roiling. Sara's mother takes Meg by the arm so they can walk together. She says, *We're so happy to be meeting you.* After the beach Meg and Sara will sit in the sun, on the cold brick terrace next to the house. They'll clean sand from the dog's feet while it stands, sun-warm, alert to something down the beach. They'll stay together with the towel rumpled on their laps and let the dog run to the fence, where it glowers at a distant point in the trees, some far-off movement. The wind whips up around them, Meg takes Sara's hand to move her closer. Her hand is small and warm; they lean their heads together. The cold wind makes Meg shiver, and she imagines what if they stayed this way, very still in low dusk light, like something dipped in amber. She wants to say, *Stay here.* The dog comes over then, nudges its head on Sara's lap, gives a longing grumble. *I'm extremely cold,* says Meg at last, and Sara laughs her beautiful, porous laugh. She wraps her arm around Meg's shoulder. *Be warm,* she says. *Okay? Be warm.* The dog lets out a short, demanding sound, as, memorably, Sara tips her face up to the sun.

CANNIBAL TRANSLATION / CHLOE GARCIA ROBERTS

TRUE HISTORY: A RENDERING

The *Historia verdadera de la conquista de la nueva españa* (*The True History of the Conquest of New Spain*), written by Bernal Díaz del Castillo, who served as a soldier in the conquest of Mexico under Hernan Cortés, chronicles the army's journey to the city on a lake at the heart of the Aztec empire, and the destruction that followed. Dubbed the first great American novel, it is part of the bedrock of Mexican consciousness, a supra text along the lines of the Bible or the *Odyssey*.

The *Historia verdadera* was first published in 1632, in a version that was heavily edited to favor Spanish interests. The true *True History* was only published in 1904, after the original manuscript, which had been thought lost, was discovered in Guatemala, where Díaz had lived out the rest of his life after his time in Mexico.

We had a copy of the *Historia verdadera* in my house growing up, and I remember taking it down a few times, reading it fitfully, never consecutively or completely, but always circling that glimpse of a city that underlaid the city that I knew. A few years ago, I happened to hear a story at a family wedding of how my great-grandfather Genaro García,

a historian, bibliophile, and director of what is now the Museo Nacional de Antropología, traveled to Guatemala, obtained a copy of the original manuscript, and republished it. This edition, known as the Guatemala manuscript, has become the standard and it outlines all the multitudinous ways the earlier version had been changed, edited, and cut.

At first, I returned to the text simply out of curiosity, to see what I could determine about my great-grandfather's personal connection to it. But then, drawn back to that first description of Mexico City, I found myself working alongside him, comparing editions, picking sentences apart, considering the meaning behind each word. Translation is the best mode of understanding for me, and I began to translate certain fragments of the text so as to better see them. Almost immediately, I regretted the narrowing that had to occur for these words to arrive in English. I wanted to reveal more. So, armed with Haroldo De Campos's philosophy of cannibal translation and its endorsement and celebration of textual reconfiguration and reincarnation, I invited my poet self to join in the work.

CAPÍTULO LXXXVII / BERNAL DÍAZ DEL CASTILLO

[THE ENTRANCE]

Don't marvel that I describe it this way here,
because there is so much to think about.
I don't know how to put it into words,
how to make you see the things we saw:
the never-heard,
the never-seen,
the never-dreamed.

———

Don't be surprised that I'm writing like this,
because I don't know how to tell you about it.
There is too much to think over,
all the things that we saw.
Things that before that instant we had never heard,
never glimpsed,
never even imagined.

———

The thing is not to marvel at what I write or the way I write,
because I have so much in my head
and have no plan for how I will convey
what was seen that had never been seen,
nor listened to,
nor even realized,
until that moment.

———

Don't be amazed at the way I am writing,
because you need to think carefully
about what I don't know how to tell you.
You need to see what was never perceived,
never witnessed,
never even substantiated,
the way that we saw.

―――――

Don't be surprised by the way I am writing.
I have to think so carefully [about it],
I don't know how I will construe it [a way]
to see things never listened for,
or looked for,
or even conceived of,
the way we did.

―――――

Don't wonder at the way I am describing this,
because you need to focus on what I don't know,
how I [will] translate the things we witnessed,
unheard of,
unseen,
and even,
undreamed.

CAPÍTULO CLVI / BERNAL DÍAZ DEL CASTILLO

[CUAUHTÉMOC CAPTURED]

It rained and flashed and thundered that afternoon until the middle of the night, with so much more water than ever before. And once it was known Cuauhtémoc had been overcome, we soldiers were left as deaf as if we had been men standing within a bell tower where many bells were ringing in that very instant when what had been ringing ceased to ring, when what had been singing ceased to sing.

And this I say specifically because for the entirety of the ninety-three days we were in that city, night and day the Mexican captains were yelling and shouting, warning the squadrons and warriors who were set to battle on the arteries; others calling to those in canoes who were to fight with the brigantines and with those of us on the bridges; others hammering, sinking in sharpened palisades and opening and deepening the waterways and bridges and making stone fortifications; others preparing lances and arrows; and the women rounding stones to hurl with slings.

And so from the adoratories and towers to their idols those goddamned drums and horns those painful tall drums never ceased to sound. And so by night and by day, we were held in this great sound, so we didn't hear one another, so that one could not hear the others, and after we made Cuauhtémoc a prisoner the screams ceased and all noise.

This is why I said before it was as if we had been within a bell tower. This is why I said before what had been ringing ceased to ring, what had been singing ceased to sing.

CAPÍTULO CLVII / BERNAL DÍAZ DEL CASTILLO

[THE RULE OF CORTÉS]

And so while Cortés was in Coyoacán and staying in these palaces with whitewashed walls that could be written upon with charcoal or some sort of ink, he would wake every morning to read the writing on the wall.

There were many slurs, some in prose and some in verse, some malicious, in the way of farce.

There was writing that said that the sun and the moon and the sky and the stars and the sea and the land have their paths, and if at any time they deviate from the inclination for which they were created, if they stray beyond its delineations, they will still return to their original state. They will still return to their original being.

There was writing that said that this is the way it is with the ambition and command of Cortés, that it will come to pass that he will become again who he always was.

There was writing that said it had to happen, this return. A return to his primary nature. A return to his first incarnation. A return to himself, who he first was.

Charles Burchfield, *Flaming Orange Northern Sky at Sunset/V-4*, July, 16, 1915.

WEATHER / CHARLES BURCHFIELD

MY PENCIL WAS FRANTIC

Charles Burchfield was born in 1893 Ashtabula, Ohio, and made his first paintings in and around the Lake Erie watershed where he grew up. In 1919, after six months in the Army, working on camouflage design, he moved to Gardenville, New York, where he worked for nine years at M. H. Birge & Sons, designing wallpaper. In 1929, he began to support himself as a painter. His reputation grew quickly; in 1930, *Charles Burchfield: Early Watercolors 1916-1918* was the Museum of Modern Art's first one-person exhibition.

He painted landscapes and city scenes, and worked in watercolor, and while his paintings might be mistaken for 1960s psychedelia, they are in fact sober and patient descriptions of fields and streams, daytime clouds and nighttime moons. Like Thoreau, of whom Burchfield was a fan, he explored the connections between the physical world and human emotion: trees exude their presence and fields vibrate with the light that Burchfield senses not just with his eye but his whole ecstatic being; as the telegraph pole was Thoreau's Aeolian harp, Burchfield painted telephone lines that both translated and connected worlds and emotions—that illustrated, in Thoreau's phrase, "thoughts conversing with the sky."

In his tireless surveying, Burchfield kept a journal of words, as well as notes on the sky, the latter including his all-day drawings: sketches transcribing the atmospheric events of the day. On July 16, 1915, when he painted "Flaming Orange Northern Sky at Sunset," Burchfield wrote: "A wonderful glorious day—my heart is sailing the skies. At sunset, several huge storms moving mightily along the horizon in a wonderful array of colors; after the sun is gone, a huge flaming orange spot appeared in the northern sky & startles the whole black landscape... My pencil was frantic."

The meteorological record tells us that on the day that Burchfield made these visual notes, sunsets in the northeastern U.S. were under the influence of a jet stream suffused with volcanic ash: on May 22, 1915, Lassen Peak, in California, exploded, what was known as the Great Eruption of 1915. In 2012, Stephen Vermette, a climatologist, collaborated with Tullis Johnson, a curator at the Burchfield Penney Art Center, to link Burchfield's paintings and sketches to the historic weather record, recreating Lake Erie-area weather reports using data from the National Oceanic and Atmospheric Administration. —*Robert Sullivan*

Charles Burchfield,
Untitled (All-day Sketch), July 8, 1915.

*Recreated weather broadcast for
July 8, 1915.*

For today, rain showers varying in
intensity will end this morning,
giving way to mostly cloudy skies,
with a few peaks of sun and blue
skies later in the day, with a
high between seventy and seventy-
five degrees. For tonight partly
cloudy skies, with a low between
fifty-five and sixty degrees. For
tomorrow partly sunny skies, with a
few clouds around the area, with a
high between seventy-five and eighty
degrees.

*The day as Burchfield described it
in his notes.*

The sketch begins with a rain that
falls straight down and is ascribed
a musical quality—"rhythm of rain."
The use of rhythm awakens our sense
of sound, of a rain with strong
and weak intensity in succession.
The skies begin to open up with
patches of blue and eventually
the sun peaks out from between the
clouds. The day progresses from
cloudy to partly sunny, as the sun
again emerges. Trees are described
as being in "alternate sunlight and
shadow."

Recreated weather report, for July 8, 1916.

Today's high was eighty and we enjoyed mostly sunny skies. As the sun sets, we are currently enjoying a temperature of seventy-five, with winds light from the south-southwest. We are also enjoying colorful skies, thanks to a veneer of high clouds and a setting sun. Expect a low tonight of sixty-five. While we would normally anticipate clearing conditions overnight and into Sunday, the category three hurricane that made landfall in Mississippi last Wednesday, while staying to our south, will bring us increased cloud cover and a period of overcast skies, along with a shift in the winds, coming from the northeast. Because of these winds, we'll see Sunday's temperature dropped by about ten degrees from that of today. We'll return to sunny skies and warmer temperatures on Monday.

The weather in Afterglow, *as described by Stephen Vermette.*

In *Afterglow,* the sky is clearly red, as the sun sets to the right of the viewer. The sky is red because the sun's rays are low on the horizon and are passing through the thickest part of the atmosphere. The shorter wavelengths, such as violet and blue, have been dispersed and only the longer red wavelengths remain to be scattered within the clouds. The presence of the moon, first quarter in this case, and darkened colors of the house and vegetation support a southwesterly view during evening twilight. The moon rose (east) around local noon and will set (west) at local midnight, thus the moon in the watercolor is approximately halfway through its transit. When the sun is low on the horizon, the sky is often brighter than the earth's surface. The sun's rays continue to shine high into the sky even as the sun sets below the horizon.

Charles Burchfield,
Afterglow, July 8, 1916.

Nov 7, 1916
Seeing the cold moon tonight I strangely
thought of violets.

—*from Burchfield's journal*

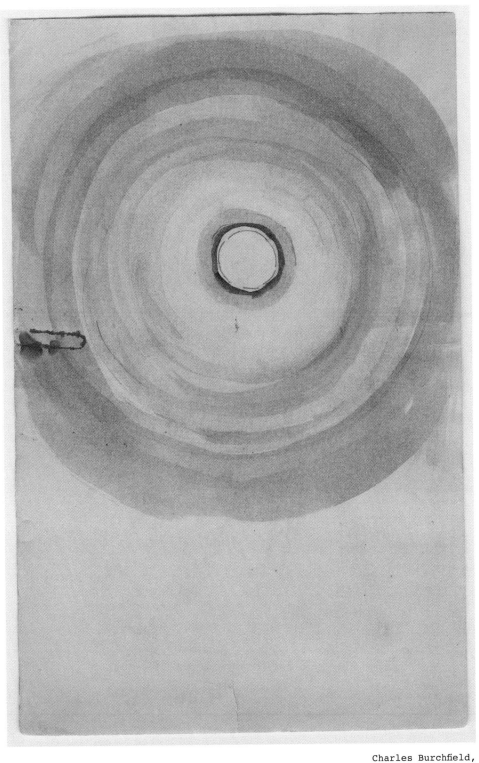

Charles Burchfield,
Untitled (Haloed Moon), ca. 1916.

CONTRIBUTORS

Hussain Ahmed is the author of the chapbook *Harp in a Fireplace* (Newfound) and the poetry collection *Soliloquy with the Ghosts in Nile* (Black Ocean). A Nigerian poet and environmentalist, he is pursuing a PhD in creative writing at the University of Cincinnati.

Kayla Blatchley's short fiction has appeared in such literary journals as *NOON, Unsaid, NYTyrant, Hobart, Vol.1Brooklyn,* and *NightBlock.* She lives in Syracuse.

Charles Burchfield (1893–1967) is best known for his romantic, often fantastic depictions of nature. He developed a unique style of watercolor painting that reflected distinctly American subjects and his profound respect for nature.

Jennifer Chang is the author of three books of poems: *The History of Anonymity* (University of Georgia), *Some Say the Lark* (Alice James), and *An Authentic Life,* which Copper Canyon will publish next year. She teaches at George Washington University, cochairs the advisory board of Kundiman, and is the poetry editor of the *New England Review.*

Christopher Chilton teaches English and creative writing at the Beacon School in New York City.

Lourdes Contreras researches Italian literature and visual arts at the intersection of ecocriticism and Mediterranean studies. She is a coeditor of the journal *Bibliotheca Dantesca* and teaches Italian language courses at the University of Pennsylvania.

Bernal Díaz del Castillo (1496–1584) served as a soldier in the conquest of Mexico under Hernán Cortés. In his later years he served as governor in Guatemala, where he wrote his memoir, *Historia verdadera de la conquista de la Nueva España.*

Timothy Donnelly's fourth collection of poems, *Chariot,* was published this year by Wave Books. He is the director of poetry in the writing program at Columbia University's School of the Arts and lives in Brooklyn.

Kate Doyle was a 2021 A Public Space Writing Fellow. Her debut story collection, *I Meant It Once,* was recently published by Algonquin.

Joshua Edwards is the author of *Imperial Nostalgias* (Ugly Duckling), *Architecture for Travelers* (Edition Solitude), and other collections of poetry and photography. He directs and coedits Canarium Books.

Indya Finch was a 2022 A Public Space Writing Fellow. She is a graduate of the Iowa Writers' Workshop, where she received the Truman Capote Fellowship. Her work has appeared in *Oxford American.*

Nick Flynn is the author, most recently, of *Low: Poems* (Graywolf).

Chloe Garcia Roberts is the author of a book of poetry, *The Reveal* (Noemi), and the translator of several books from the Spanish and Chinese, including Li Shangyin's *Derangements of My Contemporaries: Miscellaneous Notes* (New Directions). She works as the deputy editor of the *Harvard Review* and lives outside Boston.

Luigi Ghirri (1943–1992) was a photographer. Inspired in part by the Conceptual art of his time, he used his camera to examine the relationship between the physical world and the world of images. "The most important lesson I received from Conceptual art," he wrote, "consisted in the recording of simple and obvious things, and viewing them under a whole new light."

Marzia Grillo is the author of the story collection *Il punto di vista del sole* [The sun's point of view] (Giulio Perrone Editore) and the editor of a volume of experimental Emily Dickinson machine translations, *Charter in delirio! Un esperimento con i versi di Emily Dickinson* (Elliot Edizioni). She also edits *Progetto APRI,* in which famous Italian authors write letters to imagined readers.

Mark Hage is the author of *Capital* (A Public Space Books). His work has appeared in *NOON, Urban Omnibus,* and elsewhere.

Brian Henry is the author of eleven books of poetry, most recently *Permanent State* (Threadsuns). He edited and translated Tomaž Šalamun's *Kiss the Eyes of Peace: Selected Poems 1964-2014,* which will be published next year by Milkweed Editions.

Vivian Hu is a cellist and was a 2022 A Public Space Writing Fellow. Her work has appeared in *Narrative* and *Triangle House Review,* among other publications. She received her MFA from Cornell University and now teaches undergraduate creative writing there.

Kristin Keegan was a 2022 A Public Space Writing Fellow. Her poetry has appeared in the *California Quarterly,* the *Southwest Review,* and *Plainsong,* among other publications. She lives in northern California.

H. L. Kim is an English literature student at Bowdoin College. She lives in Brunswick, Maine.

Joanna Klink is the author of five books of poetry, most recently *The Nightfields* (Penguin). She teaches at the Michener Center for Writers in Austin, Texas.

Josef Koudelka was born in Moravia in 1938. He left Czechoslovakia in 1970 and was briefly stateless before obtaining political asylum in England. Shortly afterwards, he joined Magnum Photos.

Dorothy Liebes (1897–1972) was called "the greatest modern weaver and the mother of the twentieth-century palette." *A Dark, A Light, A Bright: The Designs of Dorothy Liebes,* curated by Alexa Griffith Winton, is on exhibit at Cooper Hewitt.

Piero Manzoni (1933-1963) was a self-taught painter whose work heavily featured anthropomorphic silhouettes and the impressions of objects. In 1957, he began making his white paintings—later named *Achromes*—at first with rough gesso and then with kaolin, as well as with creased canvases or surfaces divided into squares. With Enrico Castellani, he founded the Galleria Azimut in Milan and published two issues of *Azimuth* magazine.

Diane Mehta is the author of two poetry collections, *Forest with Castanets* (Four Way) and *Tiny Extravaganzas,* (Arrowsmith); and the essay collection *Happier Far,* which will be published by University of Georgia next year.

Edward McWhinney's fiction has appeared in *Contrary,* among other literary magazines. His

debut story collection is forthcoming from A Public Space Books. He lives in Cork, Ireland.

Lynn Melnick is the author of three collections of poetry, most recently *Refusenik* (YesYes), and the memoir *I've Had to Think Up a Way to Survive: On Trauma, Persistence, and Dolly Parton* (University of Texas).

Tawanda Mulalu was born in Gaborone, Botswana. His first book, *Please make me pretty, I don't want to die* was selected by Susan Stewart for the Princeton Series of Contemporary Poets. He lives in Austin, where he is a fellow at the Michener Center for Writers.

Lisa Olstein is the author of seven books, including the poetry collection *Dream Apartment,* which will be published this fall by Copper Canyon; the book-length lyric essay *Pain Studies* (Bellevue Literary); and *Climate* (Essay Press), an exchange of epistolary essays with the poet Julie Carr.

Robert Ostrom is the author of *Sandhour, Ritual and Bit* (both Saturnalia) and *The Youngest Butcher in*

Illinois (YesYes). He lives in New York City and teaches at New York City College of Technology.

Cecily Parks is the editor of the anthology *The Echoing Green: Poems of Fields, Meadows, and Grasses* (Everyman's Library), and the author of three poetry collections, including *The Seeds,* which is forthcoming from Alice James Books. She teaches in the MFA program at Texas State University and lives in Austin.

Julia Pelosi-Thorpe's translations of Latin, Italian, and Dialect poetry and fiction have appeared or are forthcoming in *Asymptote, Modern Poetry in Translation,* the *Poetry Review, Chicago Review,* and elsewhere.

Tomaž Šalamun (1941-2014) published more than fifty-five books of poetry in Slovenia and received numerous awards, among them the Jenko Prize, Prešeren Prize, and the European Prize for Poetry. In the 1990s, he served for several years as the cultural attaché for the Slovenian Embassy in New York City.

CONTRIBUTORS

Josephine Sarvaas is an English teacher and writer from Sydney, Australia. Her work has been featured in *NYC Midnight,* the *West Australian,* and *Short Stories Unlimited,* among other publications.

Mahreen Sohail was a 2014 A Public Space Writing Fellow. Her work has also appeared in *Granta,* the *Kenyon Review, Guernica,* and the Pushcart Prize anthology. Her debut story collection is forthcoming from A Public Space Books.

Robert Sullivan is a contributing editor at *A Public Space.* He is the author, most recently, of *Double Exposure: Resurveying the West with Timothy O'Sullivan, America's Most Mysterious War Photographer,* which will be published by FSG next year.

Maiko Takeda is an accessory artist and designer. Starting from the simple question of what it would feel like to wear a cloud, the Atmospheric Reentry collection is a series of sculptural head/ body pieces that blur the boundaries around the wearer. Work from the collection has been acquired by the Metropolitan Museum of Art. The headpiece in this issue was worn by Björk on the cover of her *Vulnicura* album.

Brandon Taylor's books include the novel *Real Life* and the story collection *Filthy Animals* (both Riverhead), which received the Story Prize.

Allison Titus is the author, most recently, of the poetry collection *High Lonesome* (Saturnalia Books).

Corinna Vallianatos's third book, *Origin Stories,* is forthcoming from Graywolf. She teaches at Claremont McKenna College, and lives in California and Virginia.

Kate Walbert is the author of seven works of fiction, most recently her collected stories, *She Was Like That* (Scribner), which was a *New York Times* Notable Book of the Year.

CREDITS

PATRONS

BENEFACTORS
Anonymous
The Hawthornden Foundation
Drue & H. J. Heinz Charitable Trust

SUSTAINERS
The Chisholm Foundation
Google, Inc.
Justin M. Leverenz

PATRONS
Anonymous
Google, Inc.
Daniel Handler and Lisa Brown
Charles and Jen Buice
Elizabeth Howard
Brigid Hughes
Siobhan Hughes
Yiyun and Dapeng Li
Elizabeth McCracken
Paul Vidich and Linda Stein

SUPPORTERS
Patricia Hughes and Colin Brady
Jamel Brinkley
Matthea Harvey and Robert Casper
Megan Cummins
Dow Jones & Company, Inc.
Jennifer Egan
Michael Gerard
Dallas Hudgens
Padraig and Vanessa Hughes
Marjorie Kalman-Kutz
Fiona McCrae
Garth Greenwell & Luis Muñoz
Margaret Shorr
Robert and Suzanne Sullivan
Emily Tarr
Leon Trainor

Mengmeng Wang
Chris and Antoine Wilson
Renee Zuckerbrot

SUPER FRIENDS
Julia Ballerini
Katherine Bell
Kelly Browne
Susan Davidoff
Tom Fontana
Elizabeth Gaffney
Mary Stewart Hammond
Elliott Holt
Mary-Beth Hughes
Jodi and John Kim
Joan Kreiss
Miranda and Jorge Madrazo
John Neeleman
Sarah Blakley-Cartwright and Nicolas Party
Josh Rozner
Pavel Shibayev
Ira Silverberg
Heather Wolf

FRIENDS
Karen Ackland
Claire Adam
Margaret Weekes and Frederick Allen
Sasha Anawalt
Lisa Almeda Sumner
Susan Alstedt
Julia Anderson
Sam Ankerson
Anonymous (8)
Lili Arkin
Christine Back
Shahanara Basar
Margaret Beal
Aimee Bender
Paul Beckman
Eve Begiarian
Dana Bell
Carly Berwick
Kaethe Bierbach

Robert and Ann Brady
Jennifer Braun
Nicholas Bredie
E Phoebe Bright
Jamel Brinkley
Lisa Brody
Claudia Brown
Suzanne Buffam
Kimberly Burns
Katherine Carter
Sara Miller Catterall
Louise Chadez
Padmasini Chakravarthy
Lucian Childs
Sunny Chung
Patricia Clark
Patty Cleary
Jane Ciabattari
Christen Diane Clifford
Federica Cocco
Bruce Cohen
Nancy Cohen
Gerard Coleman
Martha Cooley
Craig Literary
Irene Cullen
Lynne Cummins
Nancy Darnall

Chelsea DeLorme
Lawrence Desautels
Nicole Dewey
Kerry Dolan
Judith Dollenmayer
Sheryl Douglas
Vicki Madden and Jim Ebersole
Brian T. Edwards
Paula Ely
Pamela Erens
FabStitches LLC
Barbara Faulkner
Michael Faulkner
Teresa Finn
William Finnerty
Kathryn Fitch
Brett Fletcher Lauer
Nancy Ford Darnall
Katharine Freeman

Peter Friedman
Carrie Frye
Reginald Gibbons
Molly Giles
Jane Glendinning
James Goodman
Richard Gorelick
Jonathan Grant
Mark Gross
Jaclyn Green-Stock
Roger Greenwald
Barrie Grenell
Margaret Griffin
Ron Griswold
Christine Fischer Guy & Andrew Guy
Jessica Haley
Karen Hall
Thomas Hanzel
Christine Happel
Maria Harber
Deborah Harris
C.E. Harrison
Melissa Havilan
Diane Heinze
Joshua Henkin
Claudia Herr
HOLSEM
Sarah Jane Horton
Randal Houle
Marilyn Hubert
Mary-Beth Hughes
Samantha Hunt
Mary Iglehart
Yuxue Jin
Raymond Johnson
Tom Johnson
David Wystan Owen & Ellen Kamoe
T Maya Kanwal
Daphne Klein and Zach Kaplan
Vivien Bittencourt and Vincent Katz
Heather Kelly
Jessie Kelly
Joshua Kendall
Kirpal Khalsa
Kristin Keegan
Theresa Kelleher

Jena H. Kim
Binnie Kirshenbaum
Nancy Klein
Eileen B Kohan
Kimberly Kremer
Glenn Kurtz
Joan L'Heureux
Laura Lampton Scott
Carol Lappi
Nancy Lawing
Vivian and Alan Lawsky
Barbara Lawson
Jeffrey Lependorf
Mark Lewis
Jing Li
Don Liamini
John Lillich
Annie Liontas
Long Day Press LLC
William Love
Graham Luce
Katherine Mackinnon
Jorge Madrazo
Gregory Maher
Jeremy Martin
Nancy J. Martinek
E.J. McAdams
Robert McAnulty
Julia McDaniel
Elizabeth and McKay
McFadden
Claire Messud
Jennifer R. Miller
Rachel Buckwalter
Miller
William Morris
Judy Mowrey
Lubna Najar
Maud Newton
Elizabeth Norman
Idra Novey
Cliona O'Farrelly
Beth O'Halloran
Mo Ogrodnik
Eric Oliver
Zulma Ortiz-Fuentes
George Ow, Jr.
Danai M Paleogianni
Sandra Park
Carolie Parker

Sigrid Pauen
Perlita Payne
Sunny Payson
Samuel Perkins
Mary Perushek
Debra Pirrello
Sarah Gay Plimpton
Kathryn Pritchett
Yan Pu
Kirstin Valdez Quade
Alice Quinn
Jon Quinn
Carlos Ramos
Chicu Reddy
Tina Reich
Chen Reis
Adeena Reitberger
Mickey Revenaugh
Ann Ritchie
Susan Z. Ritz
Sarah A. Rosen
Julia Rubin
Nicole Rudick
Ruth and Kirsten
Saxton
Peter Schmader
Jill Schoolman
Fern Schroeder
Wayne Scott
Jennifer Sears-Pigliucci
Diana Senechal
Elizabeth Shepardson
Brian and Melissa
Sherman
Nedra Shumway
Murray Silverstein
Tina Simcich
Judy Sims
Gabrielle Howard and
Martin Skoble
Michele Smart
Adrianna Smith
Karen Smith
The Smith Family
Timothy Soldani
Sarah Soliman
Maria Soto
Peter Specker
Laura Spence-Ash

Helen Wickes and
Donald Stang
Judith Sturges
Sam Swope
Kevin Thurston
Alexander Tilney
Elizabeth Trawick
Rick Trushel
Brooke Tucker
Georgia Tucker
Charity Turner
Marina Vaysberg
Franklin Wagner
Terry Wall
Patricia Wallace
Marcia Watkins
Joyce Watts
Meg Weekes
Susan Wheeler
Katie Wilson
Mary Beth Witherup
Sierra Yit
Jenny Xie
Diane Zorich

"A CABINET OF WONDERS"*

GERTRUDE ABERCROMBIE
KAVEH AKBAR
LĀYLĀH ĀLI
JAMES ALLEN HALL
SELVA ALMADA
JJ AMAWORO WILSON
KAREN AN-HWEI LEE
RUSSELL ATKINS
MARY JO BANG
ARI BANIAS
BRUCE BARBER
MEGAN BERKOBIEN
MARK BIBBINS
KAYLA BLATCHLEY
DANIEL BORZUTZKY
MARCEL BROODTHAERS
LILY BROWN
DAVID BOYD
ANNE BOYER
JAMEL BRINKLEY
NIN BRUDERMANN
PETER BUSH
BRIAN CALVIN
LEA CARPENTER
WENDY CHEN
ANNIE COGGAN
KATE COLBY
MARGARET JULL COSTA
GREGORY CREWDSON
P. SCOTT CUNNINGHAM
BRUNA DANTAS LOBATO
KIKI DELANCEY
MÓNICA DE LA TORRE
YOHANCA DELGADO

JILL DESIMINI
JENN DÍAZ
ALEX DIMITROV
TIMOTHY DONNELLY
ANNE ELLIOTT
EMMET ELLIOTT
ALICE ELLIOTT DARK
GRAHAM FOUST
JOHN FREEMAN
WILL FRYER
MINDY FULLILOVE
ELISA GABBERT
N. C. GERMANACOS
TEOLINDA GERSÃO
REGINALD GIBBONS
MARIA GILISSEN
CASSANDRA GILLIG
KRISTEN GLEASON
MICHAEL GOLDBERG
MATTHIAS GÖRITZ
MARILYN HACKER
MARK HAGE
KIMIKO HAHN
SARAH HALL
DAVID HAYDEN
STEFANIA HEIM
JAMIL HELLU
JORDAN JOY HEWSON
HILDA HILST
MISHA HOEKSTRA
JENNY HOLZER
BETTE HOWLAND
TIMOTHY HURSLEY
RANA ISSA
LÍDIA JORGE
FADY JOUDAH
ALEXANDER KAN
JENA H. KIM
ROBERT KIRKBRIDE
TAISIA KITAISKAIA
JAMIL KOCHAI
SANA KRASIKOV
JHUMPA LAHIRI
EDUARDO LALO
DAVID LARSEN
AMY LEACH
LE CORBUSIER
SUZANNE JILL LEVINE
YIYUN LI
KELLY LINK
GORDON LISH

ARVID LOGAN
BEN LOORY
MARIE LORENZ
BRIDGET LOWE
VICKI MADDEN
JORDANA MAISIE
NIKKI MALOOF
KNOX MARTIN
RANIA MATAR
MELISSA MCGRAW
PHOEBE MCILWAIN BRIGHT
MEREDITH MCKINNEY
DEIRDRE MCNAMER
JAMES ALAN MCPHERSON
ALEXANDER MCQUEEN
EDWARD MCWHINNEY
CLAIRE MESSUD
ERIKA MIHÁLYCSA
CLEO MIKUTTA
STEVEN MILLHAUSER
GOTHATAONE MOENG
QUIM MONZÓ
INGE MORATH
SUNEELA MUBAYI
BONNIE NADZAM
DORTHE NORS
CATHERINE PIERCE
TAYLOR PLIMPTON
ANZHELINA POLONSKAYA
ALISON POWELL
JULIA POWERS
LI QINGZHAO
ANNA RABINOWITZ
PACO RABANNE
NATASHA RANDALL
NEAL RANTOUL
SRIKANTH REDDY
RICHARD ROBBINS
MERCÈ RODOREDA
MATTHEW ROHRER
SAMUEL RUTTER
SASHA SABEN CALLAGHAN
CHERYL SAVAGEAU
DENISE SCOTT BROWN

SCOTT SHANAHAN
AL-SHAMMAKH IBN DIRAR
FARIS AL-SHIDYAQ
CALLIE SISKEL
EVA SPEER
THOMAS STRUTH
ROBERT SULLIVAN
CLAIRE SYLVESTER SMITH
FIONA SZE-LORRAIN
DEBORAH TAFFA
ZSUZSA TAKÁCS
KAT THACKRAY
ERNEST THOMPSON
SYLVAN THOMSON
COLM TÓIBÍN
RICHARD TUTTLE
LYNN UMLAUF
NANOS VALAORITIS
THANASSIS VALTINOS
MIYÓ VESTRINI
ANDREW WACHTEL
LATOYA WATKINS
KYLE FRANCIS WILLIAMS
MINDY WONG
JENNY XIE
WENDY XU
LYDIA XYNOGALA
MATVEI YANKELEVICH
YANYI
JOSEPH YOAKUM
ZHANG ZAO
ZARINA
ADA ZHANG
ELIZABETH ZUBA
...AND MORE

*Whiting Literary
Magazine Prize

SUBSCRIBE TO A PUBLIC SPACE

Tuomas Markunpoika,
Engineering Temporality

Tiny Extravaganzas

Diane Mehta

poems

A new collection of stories from

DIANE WILLIAMS

"Diane Williams seeks to stun, in something near the
literal sense of the word." —**THE NEW REPUBLIC**

"Her minimalism is distinctive for its sublimity and its
spirituality, its ability to evoke the laws of a world apart."
—**THE NEW YORKER**

"Fiction ought to lead us to those precipices where
language fails and silence begins. You would be well
advised, with a master like Williams, to take the plunge."
—**THE NEW YORK TIMES**

A PUBLIC SPACE BOOKS

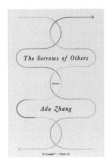

THE SORROWS OF OTHERS
Ada Zhang

GOD'S CHILDREN ARE LITTLE BROKEN THINGS
Arinze Ifeakandu

TOLSTOY TOGETHER: 85 DAYS OF WAR AND PEACE

THE BOOK OF ERRORS
Annie Coggan

CAPITAL
Mark Hage

THE COMMUNICATING VESSELS
Friederike Mayröcker

GEOMETRY OF SHADOWS
Giorgio de Chirico

THE HEART IS A FULL-WILD BEAST
John L'Heureux

CALM SEA AND PROSPEROUS VOYAGE
Bette Howland

W-3
Bette Howland

THINGS TO COME AND GO
Bette Howland